# A SPINNING BLADE OF DEATH

Ki felt a sharp stab of pain in his upper arm as one of the bladelike splinters stabbed into his biceps. It penetrated like a dagger, but the pain did not stop him from flicking a second blade from its forearm-case into his hand and launching it to follow the first.

Before the man on the bucket could trigger his revolver again the second *shuriken* reached his throat. He was starting to get to his feet when the blade penetrated. He let his revolver drop as he pawed at his gullet, where bright arterial blood was spurting along the edges of the implanted blade. Then his knees sagged, and he began to crumple to the ground. His sprawled form jerked convulsively for a moment, then he lay motionless.

*Also in the LONE STAR series*
*from Jove*

**WESLEY ELLIS**

# LONE STAR

## IN HELL'S CANYON

**J**

**JOVE BOOKS, NEW YORK**

LONE STAR IN HELL'S CANYON

A Jove book/published by arrangement with
the author

PRINTING HISTORY
Jove edition/June 1989

ISBN: 0-515-10036-6

Jove books are published by The Berkley Publishing Group,
200 Madison Avenue, New York, New York 10016.
The name "JOVE" and the "J" logo
are trademarks belonging to Jove Publications, Inc.

PRINTED IN THE UNITED STATES OF AMERICA

10  9  8  7  6  5  4  3  2  1

★

# Chapter 1

"There are times like today when I really enjoy the San Francisco fog, Ki," Jessie said.

She was standing at the window of their suite in the Palace Hotel, looking out into the grey fog. The gaslights along Market Street had already been lighted and showed through the heavy mist as twin lines of shapeless glowing yellow blobs. Turning away from the window, she let the heavy velvet drapes fall back into place as she went on, "It's certainly different from all the sunshine we get at the Circle Star."

"I imagine you just like it because we don't have many grey days on the ranch," Ki smiled. "But it is good to have a change of climate for a little while."

"Of course. I suppose I like it in the same way I do the Palace Hotel. It's a nice place to be for a

1

while, but I'm sure I wouldn't enjoy living in the hotel any more than I would in the city."

"We won't be here long enough to tire of either one on this trip," Ki said. "From what you told me when you got back from Mr. Allison's office this afternoon, another day or two will finish your business with him."

Jessie nodded and replied, "Yes, but I'm going to try to get all the little loose ends tied up tomorrow. Frank Allison is a very good lawyer, but he's like most of the lawyers I've run into. He hates to do anything in too big a hurry."

"Well, a day, one way or the other, won't make a great deal of difference," Ki commented. "No matter how—" He broke off as a tapping sounded at the door, and stepped over to open it.

"Good evening, Ki," the young man in the doorway said. Sean was a sturdy-built man and clean-shaven in a day when beards were the fashion. He was one of those regular-featured individuals who continue to look youthful well into middle age. He appeared to be in his early or middle thirties, for his face was just beginning to show traces of becoming lined. He was a half-head taller than Jessie, with broad square shoulders tapering to a narrow waist. He went on, "I hope I didn't get here too early."

"Not at all, Sean," Jessie broke in. "I'm ready to go."

"I should've known you would be," Sean Griffin smiled. "And as always, beautiful as well as prompt."

He was looking past Ki at Jessie. Her oval face

2

was set off by her glowing golden hair, which was swept in gentle curves from the crown of her head and gathered into a small bun at the nape of her neck. Her vivid green eyes were shining in the soft lamplight as her full lips curved into a welcoming smile. She was wearing a low-cut dress of watered taffeta that left her satin-smooth shoulders bare and changed colors subtly as she moved a half-step forward to greet him.

Sean did not bother to conceal his admiration. He stepped into the room and handed her the small tissue-wrapped package he was carrying, and then went on, "But do take time to put on this little corsage I've brought you."

"How thoughtful! Thank you, Sean," Jessie said. She leaned forward and brushed her lips across Sean's in a brief, casual thank you kiss before freeing the trio of rosebuds from the tissue wrapping. As she pinned the corsage on her gown, she went on, "Now, I suppose we'd better go if we intend to have dinner before the curtain goes up."

"I've made reservations at that little French restaurant you liked so much on your last visit," Sean told her. "And from there to the Baldwin Theatre's just a few steps." Turning to Ki, he asked, "You're still sure you don't want to go with us?"

"Quite sure," Ki nodded. "As I told you when Jessie and I were at the bank this afternoon, I have some friends in Chinatown that I'll be visiting."

"Then I'll see you in the morning, Ki," Jessie said as she picked up a white silk shawl and draped it over her bare gleaming shoulders. "I know how

3

late you stay when you go to visit your friends." She turned back to Sean and went on, "Now, for the rest of the evening we'll relax and enjoy ourselves."

"I hope you meant what I think you did when you made that remark to Ki about us relaxing and enjoying ourselves," Sean told Jessie as they walked down the hotel's deep-carpeted hall toward her suite. "That's all I was able to think of during dinner and the theatre."

"You know quite well what I meant," Jessie replied. "And I'm sure we must've been sharing the same thoughts during the play. It's been quite a while since we've had a chance to be together."

While they were talking, they'd walked to the door of Jessie's suite. She had the door-key ready and handed it to Sean. He opened the door and stepped aside to let Jessie enter, then followed her inside. He paused to remove the key before closing the door. Jessie took off her shawl and dropped it on a chair as she crossed the room.

Though she said nothing to Sean, the presence of the shawl was her private signal to Ki that she was in her bedroom but did not want to be disturbed. Sean had caught up with her by now. He handed her the door-key, and as she took it from him, she closed her hand over his and led him across the lavishly furnished parlor to her bedroom. A small night-light on the bureau bathed the room in a golden glow, only a bit lighter than twilight, through its shade of swirled translucent Favrile glass.

Jessie stood waiting while Sean closed the door,

and when he turned she had only to lean forward a bit for him to grasp her in his strong arms. This time their kiss was anything but casual. It was an open-lipped caress, clinging and prolonged, tongues twining and searching. They held the kiss until both were breathless. When they broke, Sean's warm moist lips traced a fresh path of kisses from the curve of Jessie's satin-smooth shoulder to the base of her throat and up its ivory length to her cheek, and then back to her ready lips.

Again they stood locked into an open kiss that went on and on until Jessie could feel Sean's crotch bulging and pressing firmly against her. She let one of her hands trail down his side until she could slip it between their bodies and press and stroke the burgeoning cylinder of flesh. At last their need to breathe forced them apart.

"We're wasting time that we'll regret losing in the morning," Jessie whispered in her lover's ear. "No more kisses now until we're together in bed."

Neither she nor Sean wasted any time undressing. Jessie stepped out of her opera pumps and shrugged her low-cut dress off her shoulders. As it was cascading in billows of taffeta to the carpeted floor, she followed it with her slip and silken pantalletes. A quick pull at the toes of her stockings and she stood naked, the delicate pink tips of her full proud breasts pebbling while she waited for Sean.

He was leaning on a chair to keep himself balanced while he finished stripping off his silk union suit. He let it drop to join the other garments that made a small, heaped cluster on the floor. Then

Sean turned to face Jessie, and she suppressed a gasp. In the months that had passed since she'd seen him last, she'd almost forgotten his masculine endowment. For a moment, she kept her eyes fixed on his ivory-hued shaft. It jutted from his groin in a full erection, with a ruddy swollen tip almost as thick as her wrist.

Neither of them spoke. Jessie stepped up to Sean and pressed herself to him while his arms encircled her. She turned her face up to meet his lips with hers as he bent to kiss her. Her questing fingers sought his erection and guided it between her soft thighs before she wrapped her arms around his chest and pulled herself close to him.

They held their kiss for a long moment. Tongues entwined. Jessie shifted her hips slowly from side to side to enjoy the sensation of Sean's rigid shaft pressing upon her. Finally, she tilted her head back and asked, "Don't you think it's time for us to move to the bed?"

Sean did not reply in words but shifted his arms a bit lower and picked Jessie up bodily. Then with slow shuffling steps he carried her the short distance to the waiting bed. He kneeled on the edge of the bed as he lowered her to the mattress, and her weight dragged him down with her. Sean started to rise from his clumsy crouched posture, but Jessie threw one arm across his shoulders to keep him from rising while she spread her thighs and with her free hand reached down to position his rigid shaft.

She was already trembling gently in anticipation when Sean sank into her waiting body with slow deliberation. Lifting her hips high, Jessie speeded her lover's measured penetration. She sighed softly as she felt herself being filled. Though she wanted to prolong the sensations sweeping over her, she could wait no longer but lurched her hips upward. With that single quick move, she drew him fully into her trembling body.

After a moment or two, Sean began thrusting. He did not hurry but rocked gently above her while Jessie closed her eyes. After she'd lain quiescent for several minutes, she began twisting her hips slowly from side to side to increase the pleasure that was growing greater each moment in response to her lover's deep caresses. The wise old geisha to whom Alex Starbuck had entrusted Jessie's sexual education had taught her well, and Jessie had learned equally well. She knew that patience rather than haste was the key to the greatest pleasure, therefore, she let Sean set his own pace during this early period of their first embrace.

Sean also acted without hurrying. He kept his deliberate thrusts to the same slow steady rhythm, stopping occasionally and holding himself buried in her willing body while he shifted his hips from side to side. When Jessie felt her lover pressing into her soft warmth, she waited until his sidewise moves ended. Then with his rigid shaft buried deeply, she wriggled her hips slowly from side to side as she lay beneath him. She revelled in the waves of pleasure that, after her long stretch of continence at the Circle Star, were now rippling more and more rapidly through her body.

Looking down at Jessie, he asked, "Now?"

"Yes!" she sighed gustily, her eyes closing as a

sudden wave swept through her. "But don't hurry too much."

"I won't. And there's always the next time. The night's a long way from being over."

Sean began thrusting again, this time with greater speed and vigor. Jessie arched her back to ensure that her lover's strokes would be longer. Sean was at the point of gasping now as he increased the tempo of his thrusts as well as their intensity. Soon both of the lovers were gasping as he continued to drive faster and with increasing strength.

Wave after wave of sensation swept Jessie's body as she rose to her climax. When at last she reached the point where her conscious control ended and her body took over from her mind, she gasped and cried out in ecstasy. She writhed and trembled while the waves of pleasure mounted to their peak.

At last a final gasping cry escaped her lips as she attained fulfillment. Then, with Sean's lips pressed to hers and their tongues still entwined, she relaxed and lay trembling. He drove with a final thrust and fell forward, lying his head on her soft white shoulder.

They lay passive for several minutes, their bodies limply relaxed. Though her lover's weight on her body was no real burden, and though she could still feel the link of flesh that connected them, Jessie stirred.

"I think a warm bath would refresh both of us," she whispered into Sean's ear. "Do you remember how we bathed and what it did for us the first night we were together?"

"Very well, indeed," Sean replied. He pressed a

quick kiss on Jessie's lips as he rose and rolled aside.

She stood up and went into the bathroom, warm water started flowing into the oversized marble tub. She waited, impatient now, as she watched the tub filling. Then Sean came in and stood beside her. He'd been there for only moments before his hands sought and began caressing Jessie's full proud breasts. His thumbs rasped gently over their pink tips until they were pebbled.

Sean bent now to let his lips replace his fingers on their rosy budded tips, and Jessie's hands crept to his crotch to fondle him in response to his caresses. By the time the tub was filled and they stepped into the warm water, Jessie's urges were once more stirring. The stirring increased rapidly, while they soaped and rubbed and splashed the warm water on one another, like children at play.

Jessie found quickly that Sean was ready again when her hands explored his body in the semiopaque water. She got to her feet and reached for a towel.

"Let me!" Sean exclaimed, following Jessie out of the tub and taking another towel from the rack.

For the next few minutes they continued their play as they flourished towels and vied in drying one another. Sean's erection had returned in the warm water with the aid of Jessie's caresses. She stroked and fondled him with gentle hands for a moment or two, then on a sudden impulse dropped to her knees and engulfed his swollen shaft.

Slowly and gently, mindful of the lessons given her by the wise old geisha, Jessie brought her lover to a peak with the soft caresses of her tongue and lips. When Sean began to tremble, he reached down and took her arm. She looked up at him with a question in her eyes.

"We'll be more comfortable in bed," he said, pulling Jessie to her feet. He lifted her and carried her to the bed. He laid her across it and spread her knees, then knelt between them. When she first felt the gentle rasping of his tongue, Jessie did not respond, but as he continued, she began quivering. In a few moments, her gentle shudders grew into a wriggling rising anticipation, then he rose and went into her.

There was no gentleness in his lusty penetration now, but Jessie welcomed the thrusts of Sean's swollen shaft and responded by rising just as lustily to meet each downward lunge. Their fever peaked more rapidly than before, and neither of them made any effort to retard its rise. Jessie cried out with joy as she reached her summit of passion, and Sean was not far behind with his last climactic plunges. He fell forward, his muscular body trembling, a soft moan of ultimate pleasure escaping his lips to merge with Jessie's gentle sighs. Then they lay silent and motionless, with their legs still entangled, wrapped in each others arms.

Jessie lost track of time. She did not stir until the pressure of Sean's muscular body on her thighs began to bother her. When she stirred and tried to move, Sean pulled away. When Jessie rolled over and stretched out on the bed in a more convenional position than before, he moved to lie beside her. Their bodies barely touched.

After they'd lain motionless a few minutes, Jessie said, "We'll feel better for resting, and the night's not over yet."

"For which I'm very glad," he replied.

"And so am I. We don't meet very often, and it's—" She broke off, frowning, when a gentle rapping sounded at the door. She then went on, "That must be Ki, but it's not like him to break in when he knows—" She stopped as the soft tap-tap-tap of fingertips on the door was repeated. Then she raised her voice and called questioningly, "Ki?"

Ki's voice was muffled by the door when he replied, "Yes, Jessie. Can we talk for a moment?"

"Something's happened to Ki," Jessie said to Sean, her voice just above a whisper. "And knowing him, it must be something very, very important or he wouldn't disturb me."

"Then you'd better find out what's wrong," Sean suggested. "Go ahead, Jessie. I'll still be here when you get back."

Jessie was already on her feet. She stepped to the closet door and took out a desssing gown. She shrugged into it as she moved to the door of the suite's sitting room. Before going out, she turned to Sean and said, "I shouldn't be gone but a moment or two."

"There's no hurry. Wild horses couldn't pull me away."

Nodding, Jessie opened the door and went into the adjoining room. Ki had moved away from the door. He was standing in the center of the sitting room, a worried frown on his usually impassive face.

"What on earth has upset you, Ki?" Jessie asked.

"Perhaps I should not have disturbed you," Ki replied. "But I have had some unsettling news. I need to talk to you about it, Jessie."

Ki's unaccustomed frown and worried manner told Jessie that he was indeed upset. Over the years, even though they'd faced so many emergencies and desperate situations together, she had never seen his imperturbability broken as it was now.

"Sit down, Ki," she said, motioning toward a chair and settling into another that stood nearby. "You know that we'll do whatever's needed to solve whatever problem has come up."

Ki started to reply, thought better of it, and sat down in the chair Jessie had indicated. Slowly, his face grew smooth and his agitation faded. Jessie sat silent, waiting for him to speak. At last Ki shook his head as though he was shedding the effects of a nightmare. Then he began talking.

"I told you some time ago of the letter that came from my mother's brother in Japan," he began. "The letter telling me that they were thinking of coming here to America."

Jessie nodded, then frowned as she said, "That was almost a year ago, Ki. I still remember, of course, because it was the first word you'd ever had from any of your family."

"Yes. You know how my mother's family turned their backs on her after she married. I have heard little of them, only that they fell out of favor with the Emperor. He seized all their possessions, and took away their titles of nobility as well. I was very happy to hear that my uncle was bringing them here."

"But you've never mentioned any of this to me," Jessie said as Ki paused.

"I turned my back on them after they turned their backs on my mother," Ki confessed. "And there was really nothing to tell you. I waited, expecting to hear from them. When I heard nothing, I thought they had changed their plans. But tonight, I learned what happened."

"And what did you learn?"

"One of the men in the house where I was visiting spoke of them. He had relatives on the same boat. My people had almost nothing left, they sold everything they owned to pay their passage. To earn more, enough to pay their way to Texas, they knew they would have to work."

"But I'd have been glad to pay their fare, Ki!" Jessie exclaimed.

"I know you would, Jessie. I had more than enough to pay their fare myself, but they were too proud to ask me."

"But you did find out where they were, I hope."

Ki did not answer at once. He had closed his eyes, and his usually emotionless face was twisted as though he was in pain.

"What's wrong, Ki?" Jessie asked, worried by his unaccustomed behavior.

"All that I could learn of my relatives is that they were planning to join a group of Japanese and Chinese to go to a place where gold had just been discovered and try to pan enough to pay their railroad fare to Texas."

"Then it shouldn't be too hard to find them. While we're here in California—"

"Wait, Jessie," Ki interrupted.

He seldom broke in when Jessie was talking, and she knew that he had something else important to tell her. She fell silent.

"They did not go to the California gold country," he went on. "They went north, to a new gold strike in Oregon. It is in a deep canyon where the Snake River flows."

"As well as I know most of the country, I don't even know where that is, Ki," Jessie frowned. "It can't be close to any of the Starbuck properties."

"It isn't. It's even more isolated than the Circle Star. I know nothing of it, either. Alex was never interested in that part of the country, so you and I have had no reason to visit such a lonely place."

"No matter how isolated it is, we'll go there and find them, there, or wherever they may be!"

Ki shook his head. Then very soberly he went on, "That is what concerns me the most, Jessie. When one of the men in the group I was visiting tonight heard this canyon of the Snake River mentioned, one of the other men spoke up. He said it would be useless to go there."

"But why, Ki?" Jessie frowned. "If you're sure that's where your people—"

Ki interrupted her again. His voice sober, he said, "The man who warned me had just heard that the place where my family planned to go was raided by a gang of renegades who killed all the Orientals panning gold along that river. Jessie, I am afraid even to think this, but I fear that my entire family died in those killings!"

★

# Chapter 2

Jessie was silent for a moment, stunned by the impact of Ki's words. Then she said, "That's hard to believe, Ki. Are you sure the man who told you about the killings knew all of the facts? You know how rumor—"

"No, Jessie," Ki broke in. "This man is an elder of the Chinese families in San Francisco. Even though I am not of his *tong*, here in America we Orientals do not recognize grudges or the ancient angers that have kept our races apart. He would not repeat gossip or rumors."

"His information should be correct, then," Jessie frowned. "But for all the Orientals at those gold diggings to be killed is just a bit hard to believe."

"He told us enough of the details to convince

me," Ki said soberly. "And two of his own family died in the killings."

"Then he should certainly know the facts," Jessie agreed.

"There were things he was not sure of," Ki went on. He had recovered his composure now, and he spoke in a matter-of-fact tone, as though he was reporting to her on some detail of a problem at the Circle Star.

"What sort of things?"

"Exactly how many outlaws there were, and the number of our people who were murdered. These are things no one seems to be sure of because the place where the raid was made is in the deepest and wildest part of the canyon."

"You must've found out more than that, Ki. You mentioned the canyon was on the Snake River, does it have a name?"

"They call it Hell's Canyon. From what my friend said, it is not an easy place to reach or a good place to be. I suppose that's why it was left alone by the first prospectors who went to the Snake River country."

Jessie nodded, then asked, "How long ago did these outlaws make their raid, Ki? Surely something of that sort would have been published in one of the newspapers here in San Francisco."

"No, Jessie," Ki replied soberly. "Since so many Orientals have come to America, the newspapers do not notice us. We might as well be invisible, at least here in California."

"You said these killings took place in the wildest part of the canyon. Do you know exactly where?"

Ki shook his head. "Not now. All I heard mentioned was the part of the river that flows through Hells Canyon. But it will not be hard for me to find out."

"Then the first thing for you to do tomorrow is to go back to Chinatown," Jessie said decisively. "Ask questions, find out as much as you can about what happened and when and where. The more we learn now, the easier it's going to be for us to locate the place when we get there."

Ki looked at Jessie and now she got the full implications of the emotions that had been stirring him while he was telling her about his visit to Chinatown. "We're going there, then?"

"Of course. Did you ever think we'd do anything else?"

"No," he confessed. "But your business here in the city—"

"That can wait until we get back," Jessie told him.

"When will we leave?"

"As soon as you can book cabins for us on the first coastal steamer going north."

"There's one sailing almost every day," Ki nodded.

"If we can get accommodations on one leaving today, that's all to the good," Jessie agreed.

"But you still have business matters to take care of here in San Francisco!" he protested.

"Nothing that can't wait," Jessie assured him. She glanced at the walnut-cased clock that hung on one wall of the room. Even as she looked at it the clock began striking three. She went on, "Now, the best thing that you can do is go to bed, Ki. Sleep for what's left of the night, be at the steamship office when it opens. Everything we've stopped here in San Francisco to do can wait until we get back from wherever our trip north takes us."

"Thank you, Jessie," Ki nodded as he stood up. "I'll do as you say."

Jessie watched Ki as he went into his bedroom, then turned to go back to her own. Sean was sleeping soundly. She stepped over to the lamp and blew it out, then returned to the bed and stretched out beside him.

Faint outlines of light were showing around the windows of Jessie's bedroom when Sean left. Pleasantly exhausted, she lay quietly in the broad bed. She watched the light grow in intensity, thinking back over the years and the events that had filled her life since the untimely death of her father, Alex Starbuck. His murder had placed her in control of the far-reaching industrial empire he had created, changing her life completely.

Alex Starbuck had been one of the major figures to emerge from the growing number of self-made men who came to dominate the fields of American commerce and finance during the years of growth that followed the bloody struggle between the northern and southern states. He'd tried his hand at several trades, including a period spent working in the forests and mines in Alaska.

On his return from the northland, Alex had opened a small shop on the San Francisco waterfront, selling wares imported from the Far East.

20

He'd learned very quickly that he could buy at lower prices and also get better and more saleable merchandise if he travelled to the Orient and made his own selections. His trips to China and Japan had been more than just prosperous, their results had soon enabled him to buy his own windjammer in which to ship his goods.

Ki had come into Alex's orbit long before the Starbuck industrial empire began to take shape. Ki's father had been one of Alex's long-time friends, an American who'd married the daughter of one of Japan's samurai families. Her father had refused to accept her American husband and disclaimed the newly married couple. Ki's father had died in a storm at sea and his mother's grief had resulted in her early death.

In his loneliness and anger the young Ki had become a wanderer. He'd found temporary homes in the underground academies of combat that were springing up in the Far East nations because of the seemingly endless wars between them. While still a young man, Ki had encountered Alex Starbuck on one of his many trips to the Orient. When Alex learned of Ki's parentage, he offered him a home in America, and over the years, Ki had become Alex's strong right hand.

Far Eastern shipping had been scarce in Alex's early career. He'd found American manufacturers bidding for freight space in his small vessel. With his profits increasing rapidly, he'd bought a second cargo ship, then a third, and with the greater income had been able to buy newer and larger ships. The War Between The States had demonstrated that the great day of windjammers was ending, and Alex was not blind to the meaning of this.

Buying a small run-down shipyard on San Francisco Bay, he began building steam-powered ironclads. The growing demand for his modern ships combined with his shrewd management and honest dealing made Alex Starbuck a rich man at a time when he had only reached early maturity. His attributes also earned Alex a reputation which brought invitations for him to take part in other ventures launched by business firms in the San Francisco area. These developed leads into other highly profitable fields, and even before he'd reached middle age, the Starbuck interests came to include banks and stockbrokerage firms.

As Alex came to be recognized as one of the emerging factors in the United States business world, those seeking help in establishing new enterprises or who were looking for buyers to take over firms in financial trouble began seeking his help. As often as not, the proprietors of these flagging ventures welcomed his offers to buy them out. Before Alex's middle years had passed, the Starbuck holdings included gold, silver and copper mines, timberlands, farmlands, and interests in such growing fields as railroads.

Not all of Alex's world had been sunshine and roses. Less than a year after his marriage, at a time when he had just begun work on the vast Circle Star ranch in southwest Texas that was to be home for him and his bride, his beloved wife died. In his grief and shock, Alex had placed the baby in the care of a wise old geisha and turned his full attention to completing the Circle Star while also attending to his business and financial affairs.

These had become complicated by another problem. During his rise in the American industrial world, Alex had drawn the attention of the masters of a secret European cartel which had set out to bring the riches and resources of the United States into its control. The cartel's heads had invited him to join them. Upon Alex's angry refusal to compromise his allegiance to his homeland, the cartel bosses sent a band of assassins to murder him in order to protect the secrets they'd confided to him in anticipation that he would become one of them.

Young Jessie, assisted by the loyal Ki, had battled the cartel for years before succeeding in bringing it down. There had been years of danger, mixed triumphs, and success. Then the final battle had ended the threat to America.

Bits and pieces of the past popped into Jessie's mind as she lay in her bed in the hotel room, watching the dawn slowly brighten her windows. After a short while, her exertions in the night's shared pleasures with one of her favorite lovers banished the past from her mind, and she fell asleep.

Jessie was still sleeping soundly when Ki tapped gently on her bedroom door. She awoke at once, slipped on a wrapper and went into the sitting room to join him. She was not greatly surprised to see Ki watching a waiter who was arranging breakfast dishes on the small table at one side of the room. It was typical of Ki to anticipate her needs and fill them.

Ki gestured toward the man and said, "I thought it would save time if I ordered breakfast when I came in."

"You've been out all night?" Jessie frowned.

"Chinatown does not sleep," Ki nodded. "And I can catch up later on the bit of sleep I lost."

"Did you find out anything new?"

Ki shook his head. "No more than we knew last night. I went from place to place, the teahouses and the fan-tan rooms, trying to learn more about what had happened to my countrymen at Hell's Canyon. The news of the killings there had spread, but no one knew any more than I'd learned earlier."

"Then you still don't know whether your relatives are alive or dead?"

"No. I tried to find the men who'd brought word of the killings from up north, but no one I talked to knew where they'd gone."

"Then we'll just push ahead with our plans," Jessie said.

"It's the only way we'll ever find out," Ki nodded. "I was so sure you'd still want to go that I waited until the steamship office opened and was lucky enough to get two staterooms for our trip."

"On today's boat?"

"Yes. It sails an hour after noon, to catch the turn of the tide through the Golden Gate."

"Then I'll have enough time to go to the bank and get some extra cash to cover the expenses we hadn't counted on," Jessie said thoughtfully. She recalled the jobs to be done from the mental list she'd made before falling asleep.

"I know what we'll need," Ki assured her.

"When we left the Circle Star, we weren't planning to go into places that are still almost totally unsettled," Jessie frowned.

"How could we know?" Ki shrugged. "But don't waste your time thinking about our gear, Jessie. I can buy our supplies while you're finishing your business at the bank. I'll take our bags with me, and we can meet at the dock."

Standing at the rail of the coastal steamer, Jessie and Ki watched the rippling waves of the Pacific vanish as they met the strong current of the outgoing tide, which was flowing in a wide expanse of roiled frothy water through the Golden Gate.

"As many times as we've made this trip, I still enjoy it," Jessie told Ki. "But this is the first time in quite a while that we're going to a place that we've never visited before. I hope you got a map of the country we're heading for."

"I tried, but it seems there aren't any maps of it," Ki told her. "Everywhere I asked, the clerks looked at me like I was joking when I told them I wanted a map of Hell's Canyon."

"Perhaps we'll have better luck when we get closer," Jessie frowned. "If we can't get one, I suppose we can do the same thing we've done before, stop and ask the local people to tell us about landmarks, distances and things like that."

"If there are any people where we're going," Ki said.

"There must be! Wherever there's a big river there are always some ranches along it and small boats carrying supplies to them."

"Let's hope so," Ki told her. "But from the little information I could get, it's a pretty deserted place."

"You were right when you said we were going to a deserted place, Ki," Jessie said as they reined in to rest the horses after the long pull uphill. "I've always thought the Circle Star was sort of isolated, but compared to this it's in the middle of civilization."

"I'll have to agree with you," Ki replied. "We've been on the trail for three days, and it's been two days now since we passed the last ranch. Except for that old mountain man we stopped and talked to yesterday, we haven't seen a soul since we got off the riverboat and left Umatilla."

"And the old fellow at the livery stable in Umatilla said that he hadn't heard about any kind of trouble in Hell's Canyon," Jessie said thoughtfully. "Why, he didn't even seem to know exactly where the canyon is."

"He may've known without realizing it, Jessie. We've both seen men like him before, who shut civilization out of their minds."

"He did say that there are three or four ranches scattered around here, though," Jessie frowned. "If there are, it seems to me that we should've at least seen some signs where cattle have been grazing."

"Yes," Ki agreed.

While he was speaking, Ki stood up in his stirrups to scan the landscape ahead. He looked in all directions before settling back into his saddle, then pointed to the cloudy horizon and told Jessie, "I think I could see a little thread of smoke ahead. Look just beyond that third line of hills, Jessie."

Jessie gazed along the ragged horizon until she found the almost invisible smudge that Ki had called to her attention. "I think you're right, Ki," she answered. "It must be a ranch, though I haven't seen any signs of cattle. But let's head for it and find out."

During the next hour they made steady progress, in spite of losing and relocating the almost-invisible smoke-smudge three or four times in the ragged hilly country they were crossing. At last, they'd gotten close enough to see the thread of smoke clearly and to be sure that they were in fact nearing some sort of inhabited area. By then, the faint smudge that they'd been using as their guide had grown dimmer and dimmer and finally vanished completely as the eastern horizon darkened.

"I hope we weren't mistaken about that smoke we saw, Ki," Jessie said after they'd ridden another mile or two. She frowned as she gazed ahead into the steadily deepening gloom. "Unless we get to the place it came from very soon, we're going to be caught out here in the dark."

"I've lost sight of the exact spot, too," Ki told her. "But as long as we cut a straight line to that big jagged crag, the one we can still see against the sky ahead, we'll get to the place where we saw the smoke."

They fell silent and urged their tiring horses to a faster pace as they cut around the smaller humps, most of them only a little higher than their heads, which rose without rhyme or reason from the broken ground. In several places they had to detour around long jagged crevasses, too wide and deep to risk trying to jump across in the semi-darkness.

While the zigzag route they were forced to take reduced their forward progress, they were soon close enough to the fire to catch an occasional glimpse of its low red flames flickering ahead of them. Their eyes had become accustomed to the gloom now. They could see black shadows of people moving between them and the fire, though while peering into its light they could make out no details of their features or even discern what kind of clothing they wore.

"Perhaps we should call to them, so we won't take them by surprise when we get closer," Jessie suggested.

"There is no need to call," a man's voice replied from the gloom that had grown steadily deeper and was now midnight-black. The darkness was only broken by the reddening glimmer from the spot of firelight, which was still a good half-mile away. The speaker from the darkness went on, "We saw you coming long ago."

Jessie had dropped her hand to the butt of her Colt when the strange voice broke the desert silence. The man who'd spoken to them added quickly, "You will not need a gun. We Nez Percé live in friendship with all people."

"We certainly don't intend to harm anyone," Jessie said into the darkness. She could still see no sign of the man who was talking to them, though since his first words she'd been straining her eyes, trying to pierce the desert darkness.

"This thing I could understand from what you said," the man told her.

Now he was close enough for Jessie and Ki to see his form, a lighter shadow on the night's blackness. They could make out no details of his features, however.

"If you had not seen our tipis," the Nez Percé man went on, "I would have been here to guide you to them. Let us go on, now. From what I heard you say, you are looking for a place to stop for the night. You're welcome to spread your blankets in our village."

★

# Chapter 3

Jessie made no reply to the invitation. Though she'd spoken first in reply to the strange Indian, she was wise enough in the ways of the tribesmen to know that the Nez Percé man would not be expecting her to carry the conversation further. In an encounter with strangers, it was the men who had full say. She waited for Ki to speak.

Ki understood at once the reason for Jessie's silence. He said, "Thank you, friend. We will be glad to do as you say."

By now they were within a few hundred yards of the Nez Percé tipis, and as Ki and Jessie toed their horses ahead in a slow walk the Indian who'd spoken to them came up to walk beside them.

He said nothing when he reached them, but kept pace with the walking horses as he looked first at

31

Ki, then at Jessie. They in turn were scanning the man through the darkness that was now almost total.

Even at close range it was still impossible for them to see his face except as a shadow, but the loose white cotton jacket and flap-legged trousers he was wearing stood out in the gloom. So did the twin braids of dark hair that fell from his shoulders on each side and extended almost to his waist.

At last the man turned back to Ki and said, "When I saw you from away, you looked to be of our people, but now I see that I was wrong. Tell me, who are you?"

"My name is Ki."

After his purposely brief answer, Ki fell silent, waiting for the Indian to volunteer his name. The man did not follow the expected custom of mentioning his own name at once, but asked another question.

"Is the woman your squaw?"

"No." Then, knowing before he spoke that he risked damaging his status he added, "I work for her."

For a moment the Nez Percé man said nothing as he looked from Ki to Jessie, his face sober, almost frowning, obviously trying to understand how a woman could command a man. At last he turned to Ki and said, "I am Wah-nella. Now tell me this thing, Ki. What do you and the woman look for on our land? Gold?"

Ki replied promptly. "We do not look for anything on your land. We will only travel across it to where we are going."

"Where is the place you go?"

"Perhaps you do not call it what the whites do. They have named it Hell's Canyon."

Wah-nella nodded. "I know the canyon, and the name the white men have given it. It is still a long day's ride from here."

"We didn't know we were on your tribe's land," Ki frowned. "Do you forbid travellers to cross it?"

"No. We Nez Percé have said we will live in peace. We are not savages as we once were, Ki. We are ourselves considered fugitives here by the whites' law."

They'd been moving toward the cluster of tipis while they talked, and by now were close enough to the fire for Jessie and Ki to get a clear look at their companion. Only a glance was needed to tell them that their guide must be one of the tribe's elders. His face was creased and crisscrossed with deep wrinkles and they could see strands of grey and white hair in the braids that hung down his chest. He stopped at the edge of the circle of light cast by what remained of the fire; Jessie and Ki dismounted.

"Can we put our horses with yours tonight?" Ki asked.

"Yes, but we have no food for them," the Indian replied.

"We have corn to feed them in nose-bags," Ki said. He turned to Jessie and went on, "If you'll take our saddlebags up to the fire, I'll attend to the horses."

"I will go with you," Wah-nella said to Ki. "Your woman can go to the fire alone. Do not worry. Our women will make her welcome and help her if she asks them."

Jessie came up carrying the saddlebags in time to hear the Nez Percé's words. She said, "I'm sure they will. But we won't cook tonight. We have jerky and soda crackers, they'll do us for supper."

Wah-nella nodded and motioned for Ki to follow him. Jessie started toward the red glow of the dying fire which cast an ever-decreasing light on the circle of tipis surrounding it.

As Ki and Wah-nella moved in the direction of the half-dozen horses on a rope picket a short distance away, the Nez Percé asked, "You have not been to the river canyon before?"

"No. This is a part of the country I do not know well."

"Can you tell me why you are here, if you have not come to try and find gold?"

"Of course. Jessie and I are looking for the place where there were many of my own people killed by the whites."

"Who are your people?"

"They are what your people call slant-eyes," Ki replied. "And some are of my own family. You must know about them being killed."

"Everyone has heard of this thing. At first your people said that we Nez Percé were going back to our old ways, but this is not true."

"Who did the killings, then?"

"That I do not know. Nobody knows."

"Such killings aren't accidents," Ki observed. "The people of my country are like yours, Wah-nella. Here in a land where they are so few, they do not fight among themselves."

Wah-nella did not answer, for they'd reached the picketed horses. He gestured toward the horses that were tethered to it and said, "Your animals will be safe here."

Ki nodded, making no effort to press his companion for a reply to his last remark. He got busy unsaddling. Wah-nella watched silently while Ki worked. When the saddles had been taken from both horses and the animals added to the picket line with short tethers, Ki picked up the bedrolls that had been tied to the saddles and turned back to his companion.

"You still have not answered my question," he said quietly.

"No. I cannot answer because I do not know. This I have told you before," the Indian replied. "But it was not our people who killed the gold-seekers."

"Who else is there in the canyon?" Ki persisted. "It must be someone who knew the gold panners had been working along the river."

"Everyone knew this thing," Wah-nella replied.

"Who do you mean by 'everyone'?"

"There are still a few people in the old town close to the place where the rivers join," Wah-nella replied slowly. "And more at Joseph's Crossing."

"What old town?" Ki asked. "Joseph Crossing shows on the map we have, but there aren't any towns on the map."

"There were men who camp here looking for gold years before our people were forced from here

35

by the horse-soldiers," the Nez Percé answered. "But I have heard of the things that happened before we came here."

"Can you tell me about them?"

"There were no other people here until some of the whites came to look for gold in the rivers. They were so sure they would find it that they built a town near the place where the big rivers meet. Most of the white people are gone now, but a few still live there. It is not far from here."

"Then this town was west of the Snake and the Salmon?" Ki asked, a frown growing on his face. When Wah-nella nodded he went on, "The map Jessie and I have doesn't show any towns around there."

"When the government men brought our people back after they had kept us from escaping to freedom in Canada, they gave the land on this side of the river to the whites."

"You don't have any trouble with them now?"

"No. We do not want trouble, Ki. Chief Joseph, who is our great leader, has told us that we Nez Percé must fight no more. We have done as he wishes us to do. We stay away from the few whites who are still living in Eureka. We know what it is like to lose our land and our homes."

"Then you didn't make any trouble for the people of my country when they came to the river a few months ago to pan for gold?" Ki asked.

"Why should we? They stayed up the river, at the beginning of the rocky canyon where the walls are steep and the river is deep. We do not graze our few steers there, where the land is all stones."

"You must have heard that someone killed all the Orientals who were panning for gold in the canyon," Ki frowned.

"We heard. But it was not our men who did the killings, Ki. The people from your country were dead before we knew that they had been killed. There was nothing we Nez Percé could do to help them. We stayed away."

"Who killed the gold panners, then?"

Wah-nella shrugged. "Who knows? Only the dead could tell you that, and dead men do not talk."

Ki and the Indian had been walking slowly back toward the fire as they talked. They reached the huddle of tipis and zigzagged through them to the fire. Jessie was sitting on the ground, three or four of the Nez Percé women around her. They were eating the soda crackers which Jessie had spread on a large kerchief, ignoring the strips of jerky.

Some invisible signal must have passed between the women and Wah-nella, for before he and Ki reached the spot where they were sitting with Jessie the Indian women got to their feet and started toward the tipis. There were none of them left when Ki and his companion stopped beside the little blaze.

"Goodness!" Jessie remarked. "You must've done something to spook my new friends, Ki! We were just getting acquainted by sign-talk when they saw you coming and scooted off!"

"It is not our way to have the women close by when men talk seriously," Wah-nella told her.

"I certainly hope you don't expect me to go, too," Jessie said a bit indignantly.

"Of course not," the Nez Percé assured her. "We are not savages. We understand that you have different customs."

Jessie had a partially eaten cracker in one hand, a half-consumed strip of jerky in the other. She looked up at Ki and said, "I was so hungry that I didn't act polite and wait for you to get here. Why don't you and your friend sit down and have supper, such as it is."

"As hungry as I am now, jerky's good enough for me," Ki told her.

He picked up two of the wrinkled brown strips of sundried meat and offered one to Wah-nella. The Indian started to shake his head, then accepted it. He drew his sheath-knife and cut a small piece from the end of the strip, then handed the jerky back to Ki.

"I will not insult you by refusing to eat with you," he said. "But if the food I see there is all that you have brought, you do not have enough to eat for more than a few days."

"I don't suppose there's a store in that town you told me about?" Ki asked.

When she heard Ki mention a town being close by, Jessie pushed aside her intention to let Ki and Wah-nella carry on their conversation without being interrupted.

"A town?" she asked. "Close by? Where?"

"North of here," Ki replied. "Wah-nella said it's little more than a ghost town now, but I thought

38

there might be a little store left there, where we could buy some more food."

Wah-nella shook his head. "There is no store. But on the other side of the river there are ranches. The Indian bureau buys allotment steers from them. Most of them will sell food from the supply they keep on hand."

"How do we get across the river?" Jessie asked. "Is it shallow enough for us to cross on our horses?"

Seeing that he'd have time to chew while Jessie and Wah-nella talked, Ki bit off a chunk of jerky.

Wah-nella answered Jessie's question while Ki chewed. "No. A horse cannot swim it or even go across it. The river is too shallow for a horse to swim, and the sand on the bottom is too soft. It swallows horses and men who step on it. A wise man does not start across a river where its bottom is of sand."

"There must be someplace close by where we can cross it," Ki frowned after he'd swallowed.

"There is. While the town was being built, a man put an iron rope across the river, at a place where the current is slow. He fastened a boat to it, and the men paid him to take them across."

"A ferryboat?" Jessie asked. "We saw a place on the map named Joseph's Crossing, but thought it was just a good place for us to swim our horses to the other bank."

"Does he still run his ferryboat?" Ki broke in to ask.

"He died many moons ago," Wah-nella answered. "But the man named Frank Smith who worked for him still takes people across in his boat."

"Then we can get across and follow the canyon along its other side," Jessie said.

Again Wah-nella shook his head. "The canyon wall on the other side has only one place where the cliffs are broken."

"What's the river like in the canyon?" Ki frowned.

"It is bad. Strong and fast and deep. The canyon walls are of stone."

"And there's no place to get down to the water?"

"There are a few small canyons that open into the big one where the river runs," the Indian answered. "But when you go through one of them and get to the river, you would find it is too swift and deep to cross."

"And what is it like above the canyon?" Ki persisted.

"If you are looking for the place where the gold panners were killed, you do not have far to go. It is where the river runs over the last sandbar before going into the deepest part of the canyon."

"How far is it from the town you told us about?" Jessie asked.

"You will ride one day from here before you get to it," Wah-nella told her. "Beyond it the sides of the canyon are high and drop straight down."

"Then we ought to be able to find it without any trouble," she nodded. "What about the place where the ferry is, Joseph's Crossing?"

"It is only a moment's ride," Wah-nella answered. "Go north along the river, you will see the iron rope."

"You've been very helpful, Wah-nella," Ki said.

"I hope we can return the favor some time."

"It cost me nothing," Wah-nella replied. "Now I will go to my own tipi. You have blankets, spread them where you wish. We will talk again tomorrow, before you leave."

"Well, what do you think, Ki?" Jessie asked after the Nez Percé had gone.

"I think the first thing we need to do is be sure that we have enough food to last us while we're here, even if it means putting off going to where my countrymen were murdered."

"Yes, that's the same idea that occurred to me," she said.

"And while we're on the other side of the river buying food, we ought to take enough time to visit one or two of those ranches Wah-nella told us about," Ki suggested.

"I was getting to that," Jessie agreed. "Whoever's responsible for those killings certainly didn't come here with your friends all the way from San Francisco. The answer's got to be right under our noses, and all we have to do is follow the scent the killers must have left!"

"That must be the town your Nez Percé friend told us about," Jessie told Ki as they topped one of the long series of rocky ridges they had been crossing for the past hour or more.

"It matches what Wah-nella told us about it," Ki agreed. "And it's certainly not very likely there'd be two ghost towns around here."

They reined and sat quietly in their saddles for a moment, looking at what was left of the town that

41

had been named Eureka. After they'd looked at it from a distance, they toed their horses into motion and covered the remaining distance to the few structures ahead. At the edge of the dead village they reined in once more and took a closer look.

There was no difficulty in picking out what had been the main and only street of the dead settlement. A mazed line of deep wheel-ruts stretched for a quarter of a mile in a more or less straight line between the bare skeletons of several one-story buildings.

Among the frameworks that remained on the long-dead street, only two still had a few boards on their walls and roofs, though none of them was fully enclosed. Away from the deserted street on both sides three or four other ramshackle houses and huts were scattered at random. Most of these had walls and roofs, and glass panes still remained in the windows of a few of them.

Traces of paint made streaks on the walls of the three or four that looked the best-preserved. There was no sign of either human or animal life in the ghost town. It stood grey and still in the late morning sunshine on a stretch of land as deserted as was what remained of the town itself.

Both Jessie and Ki gave a start of surprise when the door of one of the better-appearing houses opened and a figure emerged from the door. They studied the person for a moment before Jessie turned to Ki.

"That's a woman!" she exclaimed, prodding the flank of her horse with a boot-heel and pulling the reins to guide the animal toward the house. "What on earth would she be doing in this deserted place?"

"I don't know, Jessie. But I'm sure we'll find out as soon as we get close enough to talk to her."

They covered the short distance quickly. As they drew closer to the woman, who still stood in the doorway of the house where she'd appeared so unexpectedly, they could see that she was well-past middle age. Her face was gauntly seamed and tanned an oaken brown by the sun. A few strands of grey showed in her brown hair, but her blue eyes were bright and her steps as she walked to meet them were long and firm.

"Howdy, strangers," she called when Jessie and Ki were in easy earshot. "It's shore good to see white faces again. Not that I got anything agin redskins, but them Nez Percé ain't what you'd call neighborly."

Neither Jessie nor Ki could find a greeting appropriate to the occasion. They rode until they were in speaking distance and reined in.

"Well, damn my drawers if you ain't a woman!" the stranger exclaimed as Jessie dismounted. "I taken you for one when I seen you riding up, but I couldn't come around to believing it. Thought my eyes was going back on me!"

"I'm Jessie Starbuck," Jessie said, extending her hand to grasp the one extended by the woman. "And this is Ki."

Ki nodded and made a half-bow as he shook hands with the woman. At close range he saw that she was neither older nor younger than she'd appeared to be at a distance. He put her age at somewhere between forty and fifty, but could not make a closer estimate.

"I'm Lily Hoven," the woman told them. She kept her eyes fixed on Ki as she spoke. "And from the looks of you, I'd just make a guess that you come here to find out about them Chinamen that got killed down in Hell's Canyon a while back."

"Your guess is very good," Ki told her.

"Well," she went on, "There ain't a lot I can tell you, but you folks come on in and let's git outa this damn sun. I try not to go outside too much when it's hot this way. I'll be glad to tell you anything I know."

# Chapter 4

Jessie and Ki stepped past Lily as she held the door open for them. The room they entered took up most of the small house, but through a door that stood ajar in the back room they could see the corner of a small cookstove, a blue enameled coffee pot standing on it. The edge of an oilcloth-covered kitchen table was visible behind the door.

To both of them it was obvious at once that the room they were in took up the remainder of the house. It was almost square. A double bed occupied one corner, a small sofa placed catty-corner took up the space across the bed, and the round parlor table near the center of the room barely left room for the two straight-backed chairs that stood beside the table.

"It ain't such a much, maybe," Lily said as she

45

closed the door and turned to face them. "But it's mine. And as long as I stay here, I ain't beholden to nobody. That's the only way I ever been satisfied to live."

"It's a good way," Jessie nodded. "But don't you get a bit lonely sometimes?"

"That's something else I like," Lily told her. "I lived around too many people too long. Present company always excepted, of course. You folks look like you been traveling quite a spell. Whereabouts are you from?"

"Texas," Jessie replied. "We live on the Circle Star ranch there."

"Texas!" Lily exclaimed. "That's a long ways off, and I never did see a Chinee cowhand before!"

"It is, at that," Jessie agreed. "But Ki isn't Chinese, he's Japanese. However, as you've already guessed, we did come here to find out what we can about the Chinese and Japanese who were killed somewhere along the Snake River."

"Well, you've found the Snake, all right, but you never will see hide nor hair of them Chinee folks, because all of 'em was killed."

"Yes, we knew that before we started," Ki put in. "But we don't know exactly where along the river, and we don't know why they were killed."

"Well, seeing as how you've come all this far, I guess it's up to me to give you all the help I can," Lily told them. "Now, you folks sit down while I pour us all some coffee, and then we can talk."

Lily bustled into the kitchen. Jessie and Ki exchanged glances and Jessie nodded. In the silent communication that had developed between them during their years of dangerous adventures, they had no need to talk. Both of them understood that they'd stumbled on the source of information that they needed to get oriented quickly in unfamiliar territory.

Their wait gave Jessie time to examine Lily's house, and the glimpses she got of her bustling around in the kitchen enabled her to reinforce very quickly the first opinion she'd formed of their impromptu hostess. She'd seen Lily's duplicates many times in boomtown saloons and red-light districts during the years when the maneuverings of the European cartel had kept her and Ki in almost constant motion.

Jessie had a half-formed plan of action in her mind when Lily returned, carrying a silver tray with three cups of steaming coffee on it. She stopped in front of the sofa where Jessie and Ki were sitting, then settled down in one of the straight chairs beside the table.

After they'd sipped the coffee, Jessie decided the time had arrived for her to start digging. She told Lily, "From what you've said, I get the idea that you were a country girl who tried city life and got tired of it."

"I tried a lot of places," Lily replied, "Frisco and Leadville and Tombstone and Virginia City. I even got up to Skagway for a little while, till I got tired of my feet freezing. I was on the steamer coming back from there when I heard about the gold strikes in this place here. I knew there wasn't a soul waiting to meet me at the dock in Frisco, so I taken the time to come here and give it a look."

"You've certainly covered a lot of ground," Jessie smiled when Lily stopped for breath.

"Enough to show me that I never was going to settle down unless I just ground my teeth together and stopped sometime at a place where I'd want to stay," Lily admitted.

"But you're still here," Jessie commented. "I'd take that as a signal you're satisfied."

"I guess," Lily agreed. "The funny thing is, I didn't come here to Eureka with any notions about how long I'd stop. But even when the town just sort of died, I didn't feel like I wanted to move on. I've found out that things don't always work out like you figure they will."

"Yes, I've noticed that myself," Jessie agreed.

Lily went on, "This place was just getting put together when I settled here for what I figured would be a little while. Gold prospectors was pouring in from all over. I'd been working in boomtowns a pretty good spell by the time I got here. I'd seen how fast and free money flowed in a new place folks are just settling into. I figured I could make enough to put with what I'd already set aside and have all I'd need the rest of my life. It took a while to see it wasn't going to be like I'd planned, but by then I'd already been here a pretty good spell. So I stuck where I was, and I been toughing it out ever since."

Ki had been silent until now, judging that Jessie would be able to get acquainted with Lily faster than he might. Now he said, "Since you've been here such a long time, I suppose you know everything there is to know about Hell's Canyon?"

Shaking her head, Lily replied, "Well, I wouldn't

exactly say that. I don't get around as much as I used to when I first got here, but I reckon I've seen about all of it there is. With everybody gone now except me and a few more old-timers, it ain't likely to've changed much."

"We noticed when we got here that there are three or four other houses in pretty good shape," Jessie put in. "I suppose they belong to some others who didn't want to leave?"

"There's only two of 'em that anybody's living in," Lily replied. "Joe Freyer and Simon Umbarger's still here. They're like me, didn't see much reason for giving up their places."

Turning to Ki, Jessie suggested, "Why don't you go talk to them while I visit with Lily? We'll save time that way."

"It won't do you no good to knock on their doors," Lily told Ki. "They've gone off on another one of their prospecting jaunts."

"Were they here when the Orientals were killed?" Ki asked.

Lilly shook her head. "No, they was out prospecting. They still got gold fever, even if they are older'n I am. They spend more time gone than at home."

"But you were here, weren't you?" Jessie asked quickly.

"I was feeling sorta poorly then, so I didn't leave here from the time them Chinees passed going upriver till they was killed. I seen 'em when they come by, and I couldn't believe what I was looking at. There they were, all of 'em toting packs and sacks and bundles. They didn't stop, and I just

49

reckoned they knew where they were going because they didn't even slow down or wave when they went past."

"You say they acted like they knew where they were going?" Ki frowned.

"Oh, sure. They come down along the river on this side. I guess nobody told 'em the easiest way to get to the sandflats was to cross here and work back upstream."

"I don't suppose you talked with any of them?" he asked.

"Well, now," Lily frowned. "I sorta tried to talk to 'em when they stopped, and there was two or three that talked good enough so I could make out what they was saying. Most of 'em just jabbered away in Chinese."

"There were Japanese with the Chinese," Ki said when Lily paused. "Some of them were related to me."

"Now, I'm real sorry to hear that," Lily told him. "But meaning no offense, I can't always figure out which is which."

Ki had been prepared to hear her say something of the sort. He kept his face impassive and nodded. Then he asked, "Did you see any of the Orientals after they passed through on their way to Hell's Canyon?"

Lily shook her head. "Not alive. Then all I seen of them was two bodies that floated past. But that was a good while after the Chinee bunch had begun panning upriver."

"Did you go to where they were working, to

watch them and see how much gold they were panning?" Ki persisted.

"No, I never did make it that far upriver while they was here. You see, they come here late in the summer and stayed on through the winter. But I heard how hard they was working and how much gold they was taking out."

"How far upstream was their camp?" he prodded.

"Not awful far. Just a little ways past the place where the Nez Percé likes to camp sometimes. There wasn't no redskins around right then; they'd gone off to wherever it is they go when they get itchy feet."

Ki persisted. "And you haven't been there since you heard about the killings?"

"There ain't nothing there I'd want," Lily said. "Just rocks and water and a few scrubby trees and bushes."

"And gold," Jessie put in.

Lily shook her head. "There wasn't much gold, Jessie. Oh, there was some, all right, but it was flake gold, if you know what I'm talking about."

"Yes, I do," Jessie nodded. "It's gold in tiny grains not even as big as the head of a pin."

She did not explain to Lily that among the property she'd inherited from Alex were several mines, including two or three gold mines. As she'd learned the pecularities of gold mining, she'd encountered the term "flake gold," and had found out that it described bits of gold so tiny that they often weighed less than the grains of sand in which the metal occurred. A placer miner panning flake gold

51

in a stream might work from dawn to dusk every day for a week, and at the end of a week, be rewarded for his labor with less than an ounce of the precious metal.

"Like I told you," Lily went on, "I don't go far from home no more. Maybe twice a year I watch the river till a boat comes up to Joseph's Ferry, and then I go downriver to Lewiston and buy whatever truck it is I need. There's times when I've got to wait a day or two till I can get on a boat coming back, but it sure beats riding a horse that far."

"But you surely need to buy food and some other things more often than that!" Jessie broke in.

"Oh, I don't hurt for help when it comes to trading," Lily told her. "The men on the ranches is real nice about giving me a hand. Whenever one of 'em goes to Lewiston or Walla Walla or someplace like that, they'll stop by and ask if I want 'em to bring me things."

"How many ranches are there on the other side of the river?" Ki asked. "We'd heard there was some ranching to the east, but we don't know anything about it."

"Why, there's four or five," Lily replied. "They're all strung out on the high range east of the river. First there's the Drumstick, then the Locked O's, and on upstream a ways from them is the Two Forks. Then there's the Box Y, but it's way on further south, down past the Dry Diggings Lookout." Seeing the question in Jessie's eyes she added quickly, "That's just a big tall rock that sticks up so high on the canyon rim that you can see it from a long ways off."

"And do you know most of the hands?" Jessie asked.

"Well, I don't take you for a greenhorn, Miss Jessie," Lily said after a moment's silence. "You've guessed by now what line of work I done. And I ain't ashamed of it. Sure, I accommodate the hands on the ranches whenever they come around. It's a sight easier than working in a house or a saloon, like I used to do. It ain't something I go around bragging about. I won't say I'm proud of it, but truth's truth. I ain't much good at lying."

"Neither Ki nor I think less of you for what you worked at," Jessie said quickly.

"I sorta figured you'd say something like that, but I been a little bit dready about coming right out with it," Lily nodded. "But all that's neither here nor there. You was asking me to tell you about the ranches on the grassy side of the river."

"It would help us if you did," Ki told her.

"Well, now," Lily went on, "The Drumstick ain't got started good yet. There's just two or three hands working on it, and sometimes there'll only be one besides the foreman and the fellow that's trying to build it to a spread. He's having a real rough time."

"That's the first ranch on the other side of the river?" Ki broke in as Lily paused.

"It's north from the Locked O's, maybe six or seven miles downriver from where Hell's Canyon starts," she nodded. "The ferry goes to shore on Drumstick land, but the Locked O's is the biggest outfit around here. It stretches ten miles along Hell's Canyon and runs east twenty miles or maybe even a little bit more."

"Who does it belong to?" Jessie asked.

"Tim Vetter. He's the sheriff up in Wallowa," Lily told her. "But he don't come around much. The foreman runs the place, his name's Plub Shattuck."

"How many hands does it take to run the Locked O's?" Jessie asked.

"About eight to ten. They come and they go."

Jessie nodded. She understood the ways of cowhands. Since inheriting the Circle Star she'd had to deal with those who were drifters and good-for-nothings as well as those who were steady and dependable.

"What's beyond the Locked O's range to the south?" Ki asked Lily.

"On upriver?" she frowned. "Why, after the Locked O's you come to the Two Forks, and most of a day's ride past it there's the Box Y. I don't know a lot about the Box Y. It's so far off that I don't see the hands only now and again."

Jessie turned to Ki. "I don't think there's much question about who's responsible for killing your countrymen, Ki. From what Lily's told us, it had to be some of the hands from the Locked O's."

"That's my conclusion, too, Jessie," Ki nodded. "But I can't believe that all of those people died. I think that before we go across the river to the Locked O's, we're going to have to go look at the place where they were killed."

"Oh, I don't agree," Jessie said.

"But how can we be sure unless we go to Hell's Canyon and see what we find there?" Ki asked.

"We can't, of course," Jessie agreed. "Even

though it's been more than two months since they were attacked, we may even find one or two of them still alive. You said there were at least thirty in the group."

"If there had been any left alive, they would've come out of hiding and started running before now," Ki said. "I'm not going there with any real hope that we'll find survivors."

Lily had been listening with undisguised interest to the conversation between Jessie and Ki. Now she said, "Tim Vetter, he's the fellow I told you about a minute ago, he was noseying around here a week or so after two or three of them bodies floated downriver. He clumb down to where the panners were killed to look around."

"Didn't he tell you what he found?" Jessie frowned.

"Not so's you'd notice." Lily's lips pulled down at their corners for a moment. Then she went on, "He didn't stop by my place on his way back, so I don't know what he found out."

"Wasn't there any investigation by anyone else?" Jessie frowned.

Lily shook her head as she replied, "Not as I know about."

"And Vetter never did come back?" Ki asked.

Again Lily shook her head as she replied, "No."

"Don't you think that's strange?" Jessie frowned.

"Not so much as you might think," Lily answered. "He's got a whole lot of territory to cover, and Wallowa's a good forty miles off. He didn't even go across the river to see Plub Shattuck, like he does most every time he shows up."

"He and Shattuck are good friends, then?" Ki asked.

"Closer'n two tits on a sheep's belly," Lily nodded.

Jessie had been silent. She was accustomed to thinking in terms of the long hours required to reach other ranches or towns on horseback from her Texas ranch. The vast expanse of the Circle Star often meant that she'd have to be in the saddle for almost a full day just going from the main house to inspect a herd of steers on one of the grazing ranges on its perimeter. She broke her extended silence to ask Lily, "You think Vetter is just disregarding the killings, then?"

"I ain't thinking much of anything," Lily answered. "But I sure now how some folks don't pay much mind to things that don't concern them."

"And Vetter is like that?" Ki asked quickly.

"Now, I won't say yes, and I won't say no to that," Lily told him.

Ki could read determination in her voice and did not push his questioning any further. After a moment of silence, Jessie took up the questioning where he'd left off.

"Does Vetter come here often?" Jessie asked.

"Maybe once in a blue moon. Me and them three or four other old-timers don't give nobody trouble, and nobody much has anything to do with the Nez Percé. They've got their own ways and we got ours."

They sat in silence for a moment, then Ki said, "It looks to me like we're right back where we started from, Jessie. Miss Lily can't give us any more information, and there isn't anybody else here who can."

"Not on this side of the river, it seems," Jessie nodded. "I suppose you're right, we'll have to ask some questions at the ranches on the other side of the river before we go to look at the place where your countrymen were killed."

"I'm still not sure there'll be anything much for us to learn," Ki frowned. "It's been a long time since those poor devils were murdered. But there might be some clues in the canyon where they were killed."

"We'd better be moving, then," Jessie told him.

Ki stood up, then turned to face Lily and asked, "Do you know how we can recognize the place where the Orientals were killed?"

"You won't have no trouble," she said. "Hell's Canyon starts just a little ways upstream from Joseph's Crossing, but it ain't an easy place to get to. There's rock banks all along the river on both sides."

"How will we know the place we're looking for?" Ki asked.

"There's a break in the rocks that's maybe a quarter of a mile long," Lily replied. "The river's shallow and wide there. The current ain't so swift, it's sorta like a pool. That's where the Chinee folks was working."

"I don't suppose we'll miss finding the place, then," Jessie said. She was on her feet also by now.

"Even if you do, you'd be smart enough to turn back when you get to the place where the banks are just rock and nothing else," Lily assured her. "Because on both sides of the place you're looking for they're black and mean-looking and plumb solid. All the time them Chinee folks was here they camped at the break in the rocks."

"Then we certainly shouldn't have any trouble recognizing the place we're looking for," Jessie told Ki.

"Just look for the place where the sandy bottom begins," Lily said as they started toward the door. "But don't try to swim your horses across anyplace, not even if it looks quiet enough. The Snake ain't a river to fool with, anyways not along Hell's Canyon. Past all of them black rocks it's different, but the easiest place upstream is at Pittsburg Landing."

Jessie stopped in the doorway and turned back. She asked, "Did I understand right? There's another crossing upriver?"

"It doesn't show on our map either," Ki put in.

"There ain't no ferryboat to take you over it," Lily cautioned them. "It was fixed up for a riverboat landing, but after the outfit that was figuring to run through Hell's Canyon had lost three boats, they give up and pulled stakes."

"But it's safe to cross the river there?" Ki asked.

"Oh, sure. You won't have no trouble getting across," Lily assured him. "Shucks, you can see bottom when you've got that far."

"We'll be on our way, then," Jessie said. "You've really helped us a lot, Lily, and we certainly won't forget it."

"Shucks!" Lily exclaimed. "I bet if I showed up

at that ranch of yours down in Texas, you'd help me."

"Of course we would!" Jessie answered. "But if we're going to get to Hell's Canyon before dark, we'd better leave now."

★

# Chapter 5

Jessie and Ki had ridden only a short distance from Lily Hoven's house before she turned to him with a thoughtful frown and said, "It looks as though we're going to be able to kill two birds with one stone, Ki. Lily certainly gave us the kind of information we needed."

"And I'm sure the ferryman can add to what we already know," Ki nodded. "I feel better about this trip now."

Jessie went on, "Even before seeing the place where your countrymen were killed, I'd be willing to bet that there had to be several men, some on each side of the river, to carry out the kind of slaughter that we've gotten hints of."

Ki was already reining his horse toward the river. As Jessie turned her mount in the same direction, she said, "I'm still trying to bring myself to believe that killings like we've heard about can happen in this day and age."

"We'll know the truth pretty soon," Ki assured her. "But I can believe it, Jessie. When I was a very young man wandering around in the Orient, China and Korea and Manchuria and my own homeland, I've seen things that were much harder to believe."

They could see the Snake River glistening ahead of them now, but there was no sign of a boat or wharf or building anywhere along the strip of bank visible to them. Nor could they see a post or pier that might serve to anchor the cable that a ferryboat would require to keep it on course in swift water.

"We overlooked one thing," Jessie remarked. "We didn't ask Lily exactly where the boat lands."

"It didn't occur to me to ask," Ki told her. "But when we get to the river it should be easy enough to look up and down along the bank and spot the landing-place."

They rode on through the low-growing expanse of wild grasses and weeds that still separated them from the river and grew down to the water-scoured stretch of small stones and pebbles that still lay between them and the riverbank. At the water's edge, they reined up. Ki pointed to the ferry's cable, only a short distance downstream. It was looped around a massive boulder that protruded from the shallow water that swept in small bubbles of froth and foam along the stone-strewn bank.

There was no boat on the shore, but by rising in their stirrups Jessie and Ki could get a clear view across the wide river. The ferryboat, a flat-bottomed scowlike craft, rocked gently in the current. A short distance beyond the high-water mark of dried weeds and small branches, they now saw the unpainted board sides of a small building, not big enough to be called a house.

"It's a long way across the river," Ki said as they sat in their saddles taking stock on their surroundings. "Do you think the ferryman can hear us if he's inside that shed?"

Jessie had been looking up and down along the stream, and now she said, "I don't think we'll have to stretch our lungs calling, Ki." She pointed to the twists in the cable between its anchoring boulder and the water's edge. "There's his call-bell."

Ki's eyes followed her gesture. He saw a triangle bent from iron rod dangling from the knots in the cable. Hanging beside the triangle was the striking-rod. Dismounting, Ki went to the boulder and banged several times on the triangle. A moment or so passed, then the tingling metallic clamor brought a tall gaunt man out of the shed. He waved at them, then stepped into the boat and began pulling it across the stream.

Ki watched for a moment as the boat started across the river. It moved slowly. Its blunt end raised a frothy wave as it moved into the crosscurrent, propelled by the ferryman. He stood near the center of the craft, using the lever-and-sleeve arrangement common to most small one-man ferries. Its propulsion came from a long lever that locked a sleeve around the cable while the boatman pulled the boat forward a few feet. Then he slid the sleeve along the cable and pulled on the lever to lock the sleeve in place while the craft was moving a few feet further, its bow raising another high swell as it bucked into the swift heavy current.

In spite of the drag of the cable-eyes that held the boat to the wire rope, the ferry made a quick crossing. Ten minutes after the ferryman had started his crossing, the flat prow of the craft grated against the gravelled bank. The boatman tossed a loop of rope over the rock before turning his attention to Jessie and Ki.

"Fare's a dime apiece for folks, fifteen cents for horses," he announced. While he spoke, the ferryman was pushing out a primitive gangplank made by nailing slats across two wide boards. He went on, "And I don't help you get your nags on the boat. I ain't aiming to take no blame if one gets hurt."

"That's fair enough," Jessie nodded.

Ki was already digging a fifty-cent piece out of his coin purse. He handed the silver coin to the ferryman before turning to grasp the bridle of Jessie's mount and lead it up the narrow gangplank. He tethered the horse to a cleat on the craft's gunwale and returned to get his own steed. Jessie stepped aboard during the few moments required for Ki to lead his horse to the water's edge and secure its reins to the gunwale.

"You folks ready?" the ferryman asked, flicking his eyes over the tethers that secured the horses.

"You can start any time," she replied.

After he'd picked up the gangplank and dropped it on the bottom of the boat the ferryman reversed the lever on the cable and began to pump the boat away from shore. Between pulls on the lever, he studied Jessie and Ki with undisguised interest.

"We don't git many strangers on this old she-bang," he said after a moment. "Are you folks traveling on through, or might you be heading for the Locked O's or the Two Forks? Or maybe the Drumstick?"

Both Jessie and Ki were well accustomed to the invariable curiosity that they attracted almost everywhere they went. Ki looked questioningly at her, and she nodded before providing the answer to the ferryman's question.

"We'll be looking in at the Locked O's," she replied. "And since it's on our way south, we'll likely stop at the Two Forks as well. If it's not too far, we might even double back and visit the Drumstick."

"Oh," the ferryman said. "Just stopping along the way while you're passing through, I take it?"

"Something like that," Jessie nodded. She saw no point in encouraging further questions, for she had questions of her own to ask, and knew that Ki did also. She went on, "My name's Jessica Starbuck, and this is Ki. We live in Texas, where I have a cattle ranch."

"So I reckon you'd be looking at how ranches gets along in this part of the country," the ferryman said. "Well, ma'am, I'm Frank Smith, and I been around here a spell. Ask away if you got anything you need to find out about."

"If you can sort of set us straight on the local trails and landmarks, we'd appreciate it. We'll be traveling through country that's strange to us, and the map we've got doesn't seem to be up to date."

"You know, ma'am, this part of the country's

strange to most everbody that hits it," the boatman grinned, looking over his shoulder as he worked his lever. "But you won't have no trouble. There ain't but one trail. You can see the main house on the Locked O's from it when you're still on the road. There's a little short trail that splits off to the ranch, but if you go straight on it'll take you right on along the riverbank to the Two Forks. It's a long ways from the Locked O's, though, a full day's ride."

"With so few trails, nothing in this part of the country should be too hard to find," Ki said. "And we're from Texas, we know about long distances and faint trails. I don't think we'll have to worry about getting lost."

"There ain't no place to git lost at except Hell's Canyon," the ferryman told him. "And if you got good sense, you ain't gonna mess around in it."

"We've heard its reputation," Jessie nodded. "And if we do decide to turn back and visit the Drumstick, I'd like to ride along the other side of the river, to see a bit more of the country. I suppose there's another crossing upstream beyond the ranches, and trail along the river over there?"

"There's a crossing, all right. Not a ferry, but you can walk your horse across. That's a pretty good stretch past the end of the canyon, you'd have a real long way to go. And I hear the trail on that side ain't such a much. It jogs around a lot and from what folks say it's pretty bad going."

"There were a number of my countrymen killed in Hell's Canyon not long ago," Ki said. He was careful to keep his voice level and dispassionate as he spoke. "Can you tell me anything about it, or is it just one of those stories travelers hear?"

"Well, he—" the ferryman choked off the expletive and made a fresh start. "They wasn't nothing but a bunch of—" He became aware of Ki's race at that point and for the second time was forced to change what he'd been about to say. Swallowing hard, he went on, "I guess everybody hereabouts knows there was some killings down in the canyon, all right, but I don't know all the ins and outs of what went on."

"Not even how many were killed?" Ki pressed.

"Why, there's all sorts of stories," the man replied. "Some says it was just five or six, some says ten or twenty and some holds it was forty or fifty. Me, I don't know all that much about what happened."

"How many do you think died?" Ki persisted.

"I don't know from Adam's off-ox," the ferryman insisted. He suddenly found it necessary to peer over the side of the boat and study the river for a moment. When he straightened up and looked back at Ki he went on, "All I heard was that somebody done a lot of shooting."

By now Ki was not in a mood to give up. He asked, "And no one's been able to find out who killed those people, or why?"

"Not that I've heard about, so far."

"What's your own opinion?" Jessie put in.

"Ma'am, I plumb ain't got none. Saddle tramps passing by, maybe. I'd say that's the likeliest."

"Or some of the hands from the ranches along the river?" Ki suggested. "Somebody who'd heard that the Orientals had struck a rich gold lode and had a lot of nuggets tucked away?"

"Now that ain't likely," the ferryman protested. "Anybody that's been in these parts very long knows the Snake don't have all that much gold on its bottom. Why, I've tried panning that river myself. All I ever got was flake gold, and anybody that's ever done any prospecting knows it ain't worth the time spent trying to pan it. Why, flake gold's in such little bitty pieces that it flows outa the pan before the sand does, most of the time."

Before Ki could ask another question the boat grated on the shore. The ferryman busied himself securing the mooring-rope and setting out the ramp. He kept his head down as he worked and said nothing, refusing to look at Jessie and Ki. He did not offer to lead their horses down the ramp, but crossed the ramp as soon as it was in place and made a beeline for the shed, where he disappeared inside.

"It's pretty obvious that we'd get nowhere if we asked him any more questions," Jessie said. "And it's also getting very late, Ki. We'd better push on if we expect to get to the Locked O's before dark."

"I'm not very happy to suggest this, Jessie. But I have an idea that if you were to go in that shed and talk to that ferryman alone, and perhaps offer him a bit of money, we could get more information out of him."

"What sort of information?"

"You remember how Lily shied away from answering some of our questions, especially those that led to the Locked O's?"

"I suppose I wasn't listening too closely at times. I was trying to think of more questions. There's so much of this story that we haven't heard. I was thinking about the next thing I wanted to ask her," Jessie frowned. "But now that I think of it, she did seem to draw away from those we asked her about the Locked O's."

"She didn't have much to say about the sheriff, either," Ki went on. "And we accepted her story without trying to dig down and grub out hard facts."

"We certainly didn't dig out too much," Jessie agreed. She looked at the shed, then nodded and went on, "I think your idea might be a sound one, Ki. Wait here with the horses, and I'll see what I can find out."

Jessie fumbled into her money-belt as she walked the short distance to the shed, and had a double eagle in clenched fist when she reached her destination. Stopping outside the shed door, she called, "Mr. Smith! There are a few questions I'd like to ask you. I'll make it worth your time if you'll come out and talk to me for a minute or two."

Again there was only silence from within the shed. For a moment Jessie considered giving up her effort as a bad job, then the stubborn determination she'd inherited from her father asserted itself. She raised her voice once more.

"Mr. Smith! I'm holding a double eagle in my hand. It's yours if you'll just come out here and answer my questions!"

This time the silence was broken after only a few seconds had passed. Smith called from inside the shed, "What kind of questions you got in mind that's worth all that much money?"

"I think you have a pretty good idea," Jessie replied. "If it will help you make up your mind, I'll promise that nobody but Ki and me will ever know you've talked to us!"

"How you aiming to guarantee that?" Smith asked.

Jessie knew at once that she'd bought what they were seeking and did her best to reassure Smith. Dropping her voice a bit, she replied, "You'll just have to take our word for it, but I assure you that neither of us break our promises!"

Again Smith took his time replying. At last Smith said, "All right. I'll come out."

Almost at once the ferryman appeared at the open door of the little shed. He looked at Jessie, then at Ki, who'd walked up to join her. Then he said to Jessie, "Let's see the color of your money, lady."

Jessie held up the gold coin. Smith extended his hand to take it, but she whisked it out of his reach.

"Not until you've answered our questions," she said firmly.

"Maybe I might not feel like I'd wanta tell you just anything and everything," he said. "What then?"

"I'm afraid you'll have to let me be the judge of that," she replied. "But I'll tell you what I'll do. Between us, Ki and I might ask you . . . oh, let's say twenty questions at most. If you'll answer ten, and fill in all the gaps that we might not understand, you'll get your money."

"How do I know you'll come across like you say you will?"

"I'm afraid you'll just have to trust me. But when you make up your mind, remember that I offered you the money, and I'm not one to back away from any offer or promise I make."

"Why, I ain't tagging you for no liar, ma'am," Smith said quickly. "It's just that . . . well, I make my living here running this ferry. Was it to get out that I been running off at the mouth too much, there's folks not too far away that'd . . . well, I wouldn't put it past 'em to give me what they give them Chinese gold panners."

"A bullet?" Ki asked quietly.

"Now, I wasn't saying that!" Smith said quickly. "It just slipped out! And I ain't going to tell you one blessed thing till I'm holding that money Miss . . . Miss Starbuck's got."

"You're taking my offer, then?" Jessie asked.

"I just reckon I am!" Smith exclaimed. "There's many a month when I don't make that much running this ferry! You hand over the double eagle, ma'am, and then ask away."

Jessie stepped up to Smith and extended the gold piece. He looked at it closely before sliding it into his pocket, then looked at Jessie and Ki, his brows raised expectantly.

"You know a great deal more about those killings in Hell's Canyon than you've let on, don't you?" Jessie asked.

"I guess I do," the ferryman nodded. "Even if I wasn't there while the shooting was going on, you know how noise moves along over water. I heard a whole lot of shots that day when them hands from the Locked O's went down to the canyon."

"How many men were there?" Jessie asked.

"There were six of 'em. Four I knowed and two that I never had seen before. I figured them two was new men old Plub had hired on. Maybe they'd stopped off at the ranch while they was traveling, looking around for a place to light." Then he added quickly, "But I ain't naming no names, even was you to give me another double eagle."

"I don't expect you to," Jessie assured him. "You said there were a whole lot of shots. How many did you hear?"

"Lordy, lady! I couldn't count 'em! There was times when I'd hear maybe five or six right close together. Then they'd sorta drop off for a while, and I'd just hear one now and again."

"And the shooting lasted a long time?" Ki asked. "About how long?"

"Well, them fellows crossed over pretty early in the morning, and they didn't come back till the sun was just about to set. They wasn't talking much when they come back, and they sure acted like they'd been dragged by their heels backwards through a knothole."

"You didn't hear them talking about what they'd done?" Jessie frowned.

"Nary a word," the ferryman said quickly. "They was real close-mouthed, just like they was when they was headed for the canyon." Then he added, "But you got to remember, they didn't all cross over at the same time. They had to go two by two, like you and your friend here just done."

"I'm sure they carried rifles and pistols," Jessie said. "So I'm not even going to ask you that."

"Well, I'll just give you something to boot for your money, ma'am," Smith said. "There was two of 'em that had bandoleers loaded with rifle shells across their shoulders. Them shell-loops was full when they went over, and there wasn't nary a cartridge in any of 'em when they come back."

Jessie and Ki exchanged glances. Then Jessie said, "I think you've answered just about all my questions, unless Ki has some more."

"One, perhaps two," Ki told her promptly. "I'd like to know if those men have been back to the canyon since that day they first crossed over."

"Oh, sure. They was all back the next day," Smith told him. "Then there was two went back the next day."

"But there wasn't any more shooting?" Ki asked.

"Just three or four shots. And they didn't stay long, that next day," the ferryman added. "I'd guess—" he stopped short and was silent for a moment, while Jessie and Ki waited expectantly. Then he said, "Maybe I better not say nothing about that. All I'd be doing is guessing."

"What you started to say was that the two who went to the canyon the next day went to clean up, to shoot any of the Orientals that they might not have finished on their first trip. Isn't that right?" Ki asked.

"You said that!" Smith exclaimed. "I didn't say a word about nobody getting shot! All I done was tell you what I heard, and anything more's just guesswork!"

"Everything is guesswork right now," Jessie broke in as soon as Smith fell silent. "And I think you've answered all the questions we have to ask, Mr. Smith."

"I figure you got two or three more coming," the ferryman said. "If you can think of any more, fair's fair, and I'll answer 'em for you."

"No. We've heard enough," Jessie said decisively. She turned to Ki and said, "We'd better ride on, Ki. It's going to be dark before we go very far, and I certainly don't want to miss the turnoff to the Locked O's in the dark. Let's get started on our way."

★

# Chapter 6

"I'm almost tempted to go back across the river and head for Hell's Canyon," Jessie told Ki as they started away from the ferryman's shack. "Though I'm not anxious to see what must be down there."

"I'll admit I feel the same way you do, Jessie," Ki said. "But what's down in the canyon will wait, if it's what I'm afraid it is."

They reached their horses and mounted then reined them on to the trail south. Neither of them commented on the way but their thoughts coincided. The same thing had happened in the past. Through the years of their close association and after facing so many perils together, their minds worked in almost identical parallels.

After they'd ridden silently for a few more minutes Jessie said thoughtfully, "There'd be no point in hurrying to the canyon, Ki. We can't undo what we're both sure was done there. What we've got to do now is to find out who did it and see that they pay for what they did."

"Is there any doubt about it?"

"Not a great deal. But I wouldn't want to make a mistake."

Ki nodded, but said nothing. They rode while the day's glow ended and the sky darkened. The transition from day to night went almost unnoticed, for the moon was full. It lighted the tree-barren grasslands almost as brightly as had the sun. The trail they were following stretched ahead, the moonlight turning it into a bright streak of ground beaten bare by the hooves of horses and the passage of wagons. Only in the distance was the landscape hidden to their view.

Jessie saw the glint of light first. It was a pinpoint when she called Ki's attention to it, a speck of yellow light that for a long while grew no brighter.

"That must be coming from the Locked O's ranch house," she told Ki, straining her eyes as she tried to make out details around the area where the light was shining.

"It can't be anything else," he agreed. Then he saw the lighter streak of ground just ahead of them and added, "It is. There's the trail to the house."

Within the next few moments they reached the branch where the trail to the Locked O's cut off from the trail along the rim of the river's canyon and reined their horses onto it. The light ahead grew steadily brighter and began to be recognizable as the rectangular gleam from a large door.

Also from a distance, they could see a window with its shade drawn, but by then they could make out the vague outlines of the house to which the window belonged. Beyond the house they could see light pouring from the yawning door of a big barn. Jessie reined in, and Ki brought his mount to a halt beside her.

"Let's not be in too big a hurry to go the rest of the way," she said. "Before we get any closer, let's decide what we'll do if we should get separated."

"And what excuse we'll give for stopping," Ki added. "It doesn't have to be anything fancy, we can simply be travelers passing by, asking directions, or maybe looking for a good place where we can stop for the night."

"I suppose that's as good as anything," she agreed. "But I'm sure something's going on there, or they'd've all turned in by now. You know how it is back on the Circle Star, the men go to bed right after supper unless they've got a good reason for staying up. I'd like to get some idea of what we might be getting into."

"We'd better leave the horses here," Ki suggested. "If we run into something unexpected, we can make a run for them."

"I think it'll be safe to get a little bit closer," Jessie told him. "But it might be a good idea to dismount and lead them the rest of the way."

Moving as silently as possible, they led the livery horses as close as possible to the edge of the glow cast by the window and dropped their reins to let them stand. For a moment Jessie and Ki stood beside the animals, trying to distinguish words and voices from the indistinct jumble of sound that trickled from the window, but they were still too far away.

"Dangerous or not, we'll have to get closer," Jessie whispered.

"Then let me go to the window, Jessie," Ki suggested.

"No, Ki. The men in the house can't see through a window shade. I'll be so quiet they won't hear me, but with a little luck I might be able to hear them. Besides, there's something else I'd like for you to do."

"Scout around the barn?"

"Yes. Hands on a ranch don't usually work after supper. And you're a lot better at *ninjitsu* than I am. You can move and still keep anyone from noticing you."

"You're looking for some kind of evidence that these outlaws are the ones who killed the Orientals?"

"Of course. Somewhere on this ranch there's bound to be the kind of evidence we need to use in court against them. I want them to be tried and convicted so others like them will get the idea that there is law and justice even in this isolated place."

"That might help to civilize things in out-of-the way places like this one," Ki agreed.

"Yes. Remember Alex's experience at his gold mines in Alaska."

"I hadn't met Alex when he first began developing those mines, Jessie, remember?"

"He was having a lot of trouble with outlaws at the mines in Alaska. After he'd been responsible for sending two or three of them to jail, they stayed away from the Starbuck mines."

"It's worth a try," Ki said. "Give me about ten or fifteen minutes, Jessie. If I can't find any sort of evidence in the barn or bunkhouse or whatever that building is back there, we'll figure out a way to look for it in the house when the men in there go to bed."

"Whatever happens, we'll meet back here at the horses."

Ki started away and within seconds was lost to Jessie's sight in the dense darkness caused by clouds rolling across the face of the moon. Jessie studied the strip of soil that still stretched between her and the house. The amber glow from the shaded window created a much-diminished reflection on the ground beneath it, but the area on all sides of it remained in darkness.

Jessie lifted her eyes to the window itself, and for the first time noticed a tiny triangular tear in the shade. Through the tear, no bigger than the long side of a postage stamp, she could see an unidentifiable bit of movement. The temptation was too great, and Jessie made a quick decision. She started moving slowly toward the window.

Keeping her eyes fixed on the ground she advanced carefully, one slow step at a time. She planted her boot soles gradually on the hard soil to avoid making any sort of noise. Still, the tiny grating when she put her full weight on one of her booted feet made a whisper of noise that sounded loud to her in the silent darkness.

In spite of the almost inaudible gratings of her

79

feet, Jessie reached the window and stretched on tiptoe to peer through the little triangle created by the tear in the window shade. All that she could see at first was a dab of convoluted flesh, but after studying it for a moment she could identify it by its fold and curved contour as the back portion of a man's ear.

As nearly as she could tell the ear was only a foot or so's distance from the windowpane. Then the man inside turned his head, and she got a fleeting glimpse of his beard-grizzled cheek and the curve of his eyeball and a tiny portion of the profile of his nose. She jumped involuntarily as a loud bang broke the quiet, then identified the bang as that made by a door that has been opened suddenly hitting the room's wall.

A man's voice reached her ears, and Jessie discovered that she could understand him in spite of the tinny tone given his voice as it was filtered through the windowpane.

"Clete told me you wanted me in here in a hurry," the newcomer said.

"And why in hell didn't he come with you?"

"He had some kind of job to do in the barn. What's up, Plub?"

"I'll tell you when the others get here."

"Me and Clete's the only ones around right now. The rest of the boys ain't got in off the range yet. We're waiting supper for 'em."

"Damn it! And I got to leave right now so I can git to Wallowa by noon tomorrow! All right, Bittman. I'll tell you what's wrong and you pass it on to the rest of 'em, seeing as you're my straw-boss, or you're supposed to be. You might not be when I get back, after I find out how bad things is going to be after that damn stunt you and them other fools pulled down in Hell's Canyon."

Jessie could tell that the man near the window had been the one just speaking, his ear moved slightly as he opened and closed his mouth while talking.

"Hold on, Plub!" the man called Bittman exploded. "That was more'n two months ago! If it'd been going to stir up a ruckus, we'd've knowed it before now!"

"News travels slow around here," Plub retorted. "There was a letter from Tim Vetter in the mail that Cookie picked up at the ferry landing today. The folks in Wallowa's been talking a lot, and they're getting the wind up about what you men done."

"But they couldn't know anything, Plub! Me and the boys made sure we'd tossed all the bodies in the river, every last one of 'em! Like I already told you, we even loaded a bunch of them dead Chinks into a boat they had hitched up to shore, then we knocked holes in the sides so it'd take 'em a good ways downstream before it sunk!"

"And that's where you done the wrong thing," Plub shot back. "You ought've remembered that dead men bloats up and floats after they been in the water a little while."

"You're saying somebody run across some of them Chinks we got rid of in the canyon?"

"That's what Tim wrote in his letter."

"How in hell could he find out about it?"

"Somebody a ways south of Wild Goose Rapids,

downriver close to Buckhorn Springs pulled two of them bodies outa the Snake. They seen the dead men had been shot, so they rode into Wallowa to tell Tim on account of he's the sheriff," Plub answered.

"Damn it, Plub! We never figured on that!"

"It might not've been so bad, but whoever brung the news into Wallowa blabbed about it all over town."

"Now, why'd something like getting rid of a few Chinks get them people stirred up?"

"Bittman, didn't you ever go into one of them Chinee restaurants in Wallowa?" Plub asked. "There's three of 'em, as I recall, and everybody in town eats at one of 'em sometime. You know how folks talk while they're eating. And there's two Chinks in town that does washing at people's houses. They listen to what's said, too."

"I still don't see what Tim's got his bowels in an uproar over," Bittman protested.

"Damn it, he's got to do something, now that there's so many folks knows about them Chinks getting killed! He says the people in town are starting to push him."

"What the hell do they figure him or anybody else can do? Them Chinks in Hell's Canyon's all dead. And there ain't nobody but us boys knows for sure who done it."

"No, but I do!" Plub snapped. "You wasted a lot of shells cutting 'em down just for the fun of it! And you got nothing to show for it! Damn it, when I told you to go grab whatever gold they'd panned outa the Snake, I didn't figure you'd kill anybody to git it! Whatever got into you, anyhow?"

"We told you when we got back, Plub. Maybe you've forgot. When we begun shooting, a couple of them damn Chinks come up with guns and started fighting back. We had to kill 'em. Then one of the boys said we might as well make a clean sweep. So that's what we done."

As accustomed as Jessie had become to brutality and death during the years when she and Ki were waging their battles against the ruthless European cartel, her stomach turned as she listened to the conversation between the two outlaws.

While they talked, she'd listened without moving or shifting her uncomfortable stretched posture. For several minutes she'd been uncomfortably aware of the pains of protest that were now shooting through her legs and feet.

She'd frozen into place when their conversation started and held herself motionless while the men inside talked. For several minutes she'd been painfully aware of the needlelike pains that were now growing steadily harsher. Jessie started to change her position, moving slowly and carefully, but her legs failed her. When she released her grip on the windowsill, she tumbled backward, falling with a heavy thud on the hard ground.

Inside the room she'd been watching she heard one of the men say loudly, "What in hell was that?"

"Sounded like somebody noseying around outside. Come on. We better go take a look."

• • •

Ki had wasted no time after he left Jessie. Keeping close to the house where the shadows were deepest he moved silently along the wall to its corner. Across a stretch of beaten earth ten or fifteen yards distant the double doors of a big barn yawned wide, lanternlight streaming from the opening. The light's rays stretched across the entire distance between the house and the barn. Through the open doors of the cavernous building he could hear an occasional metallic clinking that told him someone was at work inside.

Only a quick look was needed to show Ki that he was going to be forced to detour around the exposed area. Leaving the sheltering darkness at the edge of the house, he made his way quickly and silently to the blackness that lay beyond the lighted ground. He moved silently, his sandals making the softest of whispers on the hard ground.

At the edge of the barn, he stopped for a moment to listen. Whoever was inside was whistling tunelessly now, and the recurring small clinks of metal on metal still sounded through the wide, open doors. Ki reached the door that extended at a sharp angle and flattened himself against it. Sheltered behind the edge of the door, he peered into the barn. He could see two of the stalls, both empty, and a pile of loose hay between them, but the center of the interior was still hidden from view.

Silently Ki began sidling along the rough boards. When he was just past the center of the door, he stopped and dropped to his knees, then squatted and began duck-walking. His action was automatic. One of the first principles of *ninjitsu* instilled into its pupils is that when making a covert approach to an adversary the *ninja* must be above or below the normal eye-level of the enemy.

When one more short step ahead would have exposed him, Ki came to a halt and leaned forward, still hunkered down. Slowly and cautiously, he brought his head around the edge of the door. To his surprise he found himself looking into the muzzle of a revolver held by a roughly-dressed man sitting on an upturned bucket in the center of the barn, under the lighted lantern that hung by a rope from one of the rafters.

As great as Ki's surprise was, that of the man holding the pistol was even greater. Though he held his pistol at eye-level, sighting along its barrel, the appearance of Ki's head seemed to have frozen him into immobility.

Ki moved instinctively, his hand sliding a *shuriken* from its forearm sheath. Before he could launch his star-pointed throwing-blade, the man recovered from his surprise. Ki saw him shift the pistol-muzzle a fraction of an inch to correct his aim.

As the *shuriken* left his hand in a glinting low arc, the shine of its polished steel in the lanternlight distracted the man on the bucket as he triggered off a shot. The bullet missed Ki by a fraction of an inch and thudded into the edge of the barn door beside him, tearing long needle-sharp splinters from its edge.

Ki felt a sharp stab of pain in his upper arm as one of the bladelike splinters stabbed into his biceps. It penetrated like a dagger, but the pain did not stop him from flicking a second blade from its forearm-case into his hand and launching it to follow the first.

Before the man on the bucket could trigger his revolver again the second *shuriken* reached his throat. He was starting to get to his feet when the blade penetrated. He let his revolver drop as he pawed at his gullet, where bright arterial blood was spurting along the edges of the implanted blade. Then his knees sagged, and he began to crumple to the ground. His sprawled form jerked convulsively for a moment, then he lay motionless.

Ki's moves in launching the second *shuriken* brought a burst of fresh pain from the imbedded finger-thick splinter. He ignored the pain as he turned and started back to the house, keeping well away from the lanternlight that poured from the barn door.

Jessie was picking herself up from the hard ground when the shot rang out from behind the house. She stood still for a moment, wondering if she should investigate the shooting, but the men inside were talking louder now.

"Who the hell's Clete shooting at?" she heard Plub ask.

"I don't know, but we better go take a look! Come on!"

Jessie heard the clumping of feet inside as Plub Shattuck and Bittman started for the door. They died away rapidly, then a door slammed in the distance. After a moment, their voices sounded again but at too great a distance for her to make out what they were saying. She was starting toward the corner of the house when she and Ki almost collided.

"Let's get away from here, Jessie!" he said urgently. "I had to kill one of the outlaws in the barn. Those who're left will be sure to search for—"

"There are only two," Jessie broke in as they started for their horses. "But you're right, Ki, a retreat's in order. We've found out what we needed to know. I overheard enough while two of those men were talking to be sure they're the ones who killed the Orientals in Hell's Canyon."

"Then suppose we just backtrack to the ferry," Ki suggested. "And from there down into the canyon."

"Yes," Jessie agreed. "I think we need to know as much as possible about those murders before we make another move."

★

# Chapter 7

Jessie and Ki had reached the horses while they talked. They swung into their saddles and reined the animals toward the road. When they looked back, they could see two men silhouetted in the span of light between the house and the barn. They were standing face to face and one or another gesticulated now and then, but they gave no indication that they were about to saddle up and ride in pursuit.

"It'll be easy for us to keep an eye on them until we get to the road," Jessie said. "If they start after us we'll have a good lead. We can decide whether we want to keep going or stop and fight."

"I wonder where the rest of them are," Ki said. "From what that ferryman told us, there ought to be more than just those two."

"There are more, Ki. They're late coming in. I

heard those two say so while I was looking through that window."

"Then we needn't be in a hurry," Ki said. "If that's the case, let's stop up the road a ways, so you can pull out this splinter of wood that's lodged in my arm."

"You're hurt? Why didn't you tell me?"

"It doesn't bother me all that much, Jessie. I can ride without any trouble, but the sooner I'm rid of it, the better."

"What happened?" she asked. "I didn't notice anything."

"You heard the shot from the barn, didn't you?"

"Yes. I was afraid something might've happened to you, but you got to the house so fast that I just assumed you hadn't been hit."

"I wasn't hit by a bullet, Jessie. The outlaw in the barn did take a shot at me, but missed. His slug hit the edge of the door I was standing by and tore off a pretty good-sized splinter that stabbed into my arm."

"If those two men were going to chase us, we'd have heard their horses by now," Jessie said. "Let's stop right here, and I'll see what I can do."

They reined in, and Jessie suggested, "Let's dismount, Ki. If that piece of wood is very big, it's going to be a little bit of a job for me to pull it out."

"No, it should not be!" Ki said. "But I will dismount and stand beside you to give you better leverage. You remember the principles I've taught you of *tameshiwari* and *yau*, Jessie. All that you need to do is use them."

"Yes, but I've never used them before. But I've

never been in this kind of situation, either."

"Keep two things in your mind," Ki went on. "I summon *yau* and close my mind to pain. That's what I've been doing from time to time since the splinter drove into my arm. You take hold of the splinter and pull it out. There's enough sticking out of my shoulder to let you grasp it tightly. Pull quickly, one long firm move."

"I remember what you've taught me, Ki. I know I'll need to work fast," she said as she watched Ki dismounting.

Ki stepped up to the side of Jessie's horse and turned his side toward her. Even in the darkness she could see the protruding end of the big splinter now. It was triangular-shaped, almost as big as her fore-finger, and protruded five or six inches below Ki's left shoulder.

"I will use *yau* to keep from feeling the pain," Ki went on. "Then if you move as fast as you can and with all your strength, *tameshiwari* will let you pull the splinter free with one sudden jerk."

"If you say so," Jessie agreed, trying to keep the doubt in her mind from showing in her voice.

Ki was in position now. His feet were spread apart, his arms dangled loosely down his sides. He looked up at Jessie and asked, "Are you ready?"

"As ready as I'll ever be."

"Then get a firm hold on the splinter and count to three. I will be in *yau* when you pull it out."

Clenching her jaw, Jessie leaned forward and locked her strong hand around the splinter. The edge of her hand pressed lightly on his jacket. She began counting silently, and at the count of three, she pulled upward with all the strength and speed that she could command.

To her surprise, the long thin triangle of wood slipped out of Ki's flesh. With an involuntary sigh of relief she relaxed in her saddle and sat looking at the splinter. Two to three inches of its needle-sharp tip were stained with Ki's blood.

"Did I hurt you?" she asked.

"Only a small pain," Ki replied. His voice was level and unruffled as he looked up at her, but she saw that he'd brought up his right hand and was clasping it over the area where the sliver of wood had protruded.

"I've got some arnica buds in my saddlebag, Ki. Would it help if I crumbled one of them over the wound in your shoulder?"

Ki shook his head as he replied, "I won't need anything, Jessie. I'll just keep pressing on the place, and the bleeding will stop soon. Besides that, we don't have any time to waste. Those outlaws might be following us right now."

"We'll go on, then," she said.

Ki swung back up into his saddle, and they began moving, retracing the now familiar route they'd followed on the way from Joseph's Crossing. They kept listening for the hoofbeats that would mean the outlaws from the Locked O's were following them, but the stillness of the night remained unbroken except for the occasional whisper-faint rushing noise of the swift-flowing Snake River as it gushed through Hell's Canyon.

$\bullet \quad \bullet \quad \bullet$

"I got to say you two sure turned around and got back here a lot sooner'n I'd looked to see you," Frank Smith said when Jessie and Ki pulled up their horses at Joseph's Landing in the pale dawn.

"We decided to follow the other side of the river," Jessie told him quickly.

"Well, whichever side you take you'll find the going's just about as rough," Smith remarked, setting the boarding-ramp in place. "And I reckon it's your business if you feel like paying another fare."

Jessie crossed first. The ferryman tried twice to begin a conversation with her, but gave up when she replied to him with monosyllables. Ki had no small-talk to exchange, either. Frank Smith stood watching them, scratching his head, as they reined their horses away and left after waving a wordless good-bye.

"In this deserted country, there's not much of a chance for us to travel from one place to another without our moves becoming public property," Jessie commented when they were out of the ferryman's hearing. "And I'm sure those men at the Locked O's will follow us."

"For revenge, if nothing else," Ki agreed. "But I'm sure it's going to take them at least a little bit of time to figure out which way we went when we left."

"Ever since we started back, I've been trying to figure out what our best move is after we get through checking over the place in Hell's Canyon where the Orientals were killed," Jessie went on. "You know how these little isolated towns are, Ki. If you breathe a word to anybody, everybody else knows within an hour what you said, and some even know why you said it."

"Since the sheriff seems to be involved in this, I suppose we'll have to get to the nearest U.S. Marshal's office," Ki said. "It's too bad Denver's so far away."

"Yes, it is," Jessie agreed. "We could use the help Longarm would be able to give us right about now. I suppose we'll have to go all the way to Salem and get help from the governor."

"We can put off deciding about that until we've looked at the place where those poor relatives of mine were killed," Ki went on. "Even though I know it's useless, I'm still holding on to a tiny bit of hope that all the stories we've heard are exaggerated and that we'll find somebody alive."

"We'll just have to see what we find before we can make any sensible plans," Jessie told him. They'd been traveling on a section of the trail that serpentined across an increasingly barren landscape. She glanced at the terrain ahead and went on, "I think we're getting into Hell's Canyon now. Look how the river's changing."

It was indeed changing in a remarkable way. The Snake was no longer a wide friendly stream of relatively smooth-surfaced water. It was narrowing now and bits of froth undulated on its roiling surface. The river's banks were steeper and ahead Jessie and Ki could catch glimpses of long stretches where the river ran through barren expanses of stone so dark-hued that it was almost black.

Ahead, the trees no longer towered high. Their trunks were smaller, their tops lower, and they were spaced further apart. Outcrops of the same ebon-hued stone broke through the thinning prairie grass that further back had covered the earth with its thick knee-high growth. The trees were thinner and seemed to be stunted in comparison with those through which the narrow path had meandered earlier. Between them there was no longer grassy loam, but wide expanses of sandy soil.

"I think we're in Hell's Canyon now," Jessie told Ki. "Or just about to go into it."

Ki glanced up at the midday sun and nodded. "We've been riding pretty steadily since we left the ferry. It's about time for us to be getting into the canyon."

"I'd like it better if we knew exactly where we were going," Jessie frowned. "This country's not like any I've ever seen before. It's all pretty much alike, but it keeps on changing." She smiled and shook her head, then went on, "I think we both need some rest and sleep, Ki, because I'm saying things that don't make much sense."

"We should be able to stop and rest by now," Ki replied. "If those outlaws from the Locked O's were following us, they'd have caught up with us long before now. Let's look for a good place up ahead, and stop for a little while."

They rode on in silence, following the faint trail that grew even fainter as it led them down a long slope into the downstream end of Hell's Canyon. The more Jessie and Ki saw of the canyon, the better they appreciated its name. The trail twisted around huge jagged-edged expanses of dark-hued rock that stretched between narrow strips of viable soil.

Where there was even a thin cover of soil, stunted wide-spaced bushes broke through. There were fewer trees rising now between the increasingly scant ground cover of grasses and brushy undergrowth, and the trees were further from the streambed. Closer to the bank the vegetation vanished entirely and the now almost constant expanses of whaleback-humped forbiddingly black striated rock formed the stream's banks.

As Jessie and Ki rode on, they noticed that the character of the river's water had undergone the same kind of subtle change that they were seeing along its bank. The water no longer chuckled in the streambed, but kept up a growling broken mutter that grated on their ears. No sound except the constant broken murmur of the rushing current broke the noonday stillness. No birds sang, no insects chirped, none of the gauze-winged flying insects that are common to streams flitted over the river's surface.

In the stream, the water was darker now. The patches of frothy bubbles that floated on its roiled surface were no longer streaks of white, but brownish-yellow. They formed, floated for a few yards, and were swallowed in one of the ripples that broke the river's flow. A constant muted growling of the restless current filled the air.

"I'm getting a little bit tired now, Ki," Jessie said. "And I know you must be, too. Suppose we stop at the next place where there's anything except rocks and rest for a while."

"That'll suit me fine," Ki replied. "I've been looking for a place where we can stop, but so far I haven't seen one."

"We'll push ahead a little bit further," Jessie went on. "But the horses need rest just as badly as we do. If we hadn't been on this long downgrade, we'd have had to stop before now."

"They need water, too, I'd imagine," Ki nodded. "But I'm sure there's someplace ahead that's more pleasant, where we'll be more comfortable than we'll be here on these black rocks."

They rode on for another half-mile. The sun was no longer directly overhead but was beginning to drop to the west when they noticed a subtle change in the river's constant growl. It grew gentler, the surface no longer roiled, but ran smooth except for an occasional riffling ripple. Then these vanished, and the surface grew glass-smooth. It also grew wider very suddenly. The forbidding black basalt that had lined its banks took a sudden downward slant and disappeared under a smooth coating of fine sandy soil.

"This is the kind of place we've been looking for!" Jessie exclaimed. "There aren't any trees close to the bank, but look over there."

She was pointing as she spoke. Ki looked in the direction she was indicating. Fifty or sixty yards from the smooth light yellow sand that now covered the banks on both sides of the stream he saw a stand of stunted trees, their leaves fluttering gently in the light breezes that passed over now and then. A few straggly stunted bushes grew in the spaces between the trees.

"It looks like we've found a good place to stop at last," Ki agreed. "And a place where we can water the horses, too."

They reined in and dismounted. Their legs were stiff after so many hours in the saddle, and for the first few minutes Jessie and Ki walked aimlessly around, moving up and down beside the big slick the river formed, examining their surroundings more closely. The stiffness and cramping in their legs faded after they'd walked a while. Jessie glanced from the river toward the stunted trees and bushes on the border of the expanse of sand, and turned back to Ki.

"Suppose I walk over to those trees and look for a good place to rest," she suggested. "You can water the horses while I'm looking. Then we'll have a bite to eat. We'd better take time to sleep for a little while, too, before we go on."

"I'm sure this is the best spot we're likely to run into," Ki agreed. "Go ahead, Jessie. I'll join you in just a few minutes."

Ki led the horses to the edge of the stream. Here the water flowed over a bottom of clean white sand. The streambed sloped gently away from the bank as far as Ki could see. He took the bits from the horses' mouths and pulled their headstalls off, then let them step into the stream fetlock deep where they lowered their heads to drink.

As far as Ki could see, the riverbottom was sandy. Here the Snake was three or four times as wide as it had been only a short distance downriver. It formed a wide oval pool bigger than many lakes in the area, and from the gentle slope of the undisturbed sand on its bottom Ki guessed that the huge pool had virtually no current.

Ki glanced upriver. A half-mile away the shoulders of Hell's Canyon's black rock sides rose again on both banks. There the pool ended and white froth stretched across the surface of the river. Beyond that point the high black basalt banks recurred and stretched as far as he could see into another narrow canyon or deep gorge. Like the rapids that had formed most of the downstream section of the river they'd been following, this part also ran wild in a maze of currents and crosscurrents that forced the water into a boil of splashing waves covered with white spume, which was tossed into the air like snow falling up instead of downward.

In the shallows beside him the horses had raised their heads now. Ki replaced the headstalls and bits and gave a gentle tug to their reins. They turned without protest, then he led them across the sand to the line of brush and trees where the sand ended.

"I've been wishing you'd get here," Jessie told him. She was sitting under one of the straggly stunted trees where the sandy expanse ended and the vegetation began to take over. "I've been getting hungrier by the minute, and I didn't think to take the saddlebags with me."

"It's still jerky and soda crackers," Ki said as he carried the saddlebags to where Jessie was sitting and then hunkered down beside her.

"But at least we can eat in peace, without having to worry about outlaws for a little while," she told him as she unwrapped the oiled silk that protected the food packets.

They began eating in the manner to which they'd grown accustomed in so many other wilderness areas, biting off a mouthful from a stick of jerky to chew with a piece snapped from a cracker. Both were hungry after their long night and the full half-day they'd spent in the saddle. As they ate, Ki surveyed their surroundings just as Jessie had a short time earlier.

"We may have come further upstream than we realized when we stopped, Jessie," he said after a few moments of observation. "All the accounts that we've had of the place where those poor devils were slaughtered fit this spot pretty well."

"If there'd been a fairly large number of people here for any length of time, we'd surely see some traces of it," Jessie told him. "They'd've cooked over campfires, I'm sure. And if they were panning for gold they'd have a sluice of some kind. There aren't any signs like that around here."

"No," Ki agreed. "But suppose the men who killed them were shrewd enough to wipe out the signs their victims had left?"

"It's possible, I suppose," Jessie nodded. "I'm sure they'd just throw the bodies in the river. After they'd been tossed around in the rapids we've passed, there wouldn't be much left to wash downstream to the next town of any size."

"And hiding the odds and ends of clothing and cooking utensils and personal things would be easy in this sand," Ki said.

"Or in this wooded area beyond the sand," Jessie added.

"Perhaps it'd be a good idea for us to scout

around a bit," Ki suggested. "I think we were both too groggy to be thinking well when we first stopped. It's just occurred to me that this is the first likely place we've seen for gold panning."

"It is, at that," Jessie nodded. She rose to her feet as she said, "Come on, Ki. Let's go have a look in the trees first. Then we'll come back and go over this sandy stretch."

Walking a few feet apart, Jessie and Ki started up the gentle slope that led farther in to the ragged line of trees and brush. At close range it was obvious to them that they were not looking at virgin woodland. Concealed by the growth of weeds and low, ground-hugging bushes was an area where heaps of dried branches had been piled, spaced a few yards apart, though in no pattern that they could discern.

"That's not natural," Ki told Jessie. "People have made those piles of tree-limbs." He stopped at the first of the low heaps and pulled the branches aside. Then he called, "Jessie! Come look at this!"

Jessie hurried to join him. She stopped beside him and looked into the shallow pit. Its sides and ends had been lined with flat stones, and a heap of tousselled clothing was strewn on its bottom.

"It's a bed-shelter!" Ki said. "Almost exactly like the ones I saw the peasants using many years ago, when I was on Okinawa!"

"Then this is an Oriental way of sleeping?" Jessie asked.

"On farms, yes," Ki nodded. "Where the land-owner doesn't provide sleeping-huts for his peasants, they dig pits like these to sleep in during the cold nights."

"So we're in the right place," Jessie said. "It's a good thing that I—"

She stopped short when a faint voice reached their ears. It was so thin and weak that it was little louder than a breeze rustling the branches of the nearby trees.

"Please!" the speaker said. "Help me! Help me before I am dead!"

# Chapter 8

For a moment both Jessie and Ki stood in frozen surprise. Then the voice sounded again, a whisper little louder than the hushed sound of the light breeze rustling the tree-limbs.

"Here!" it said. "I am here! But I cannot move! Help me or I will die!"

Ki had been waiting for the anguished plea to be repeated, and this time he managed to locate the general area from which the plea had come. He hurried to a low pile of brush only a few steps away and began tossing the dead branches aside. Jessie ran to join him, and only a few moments were required for them to uncover the bed-shelter. They looked into the pit, ignoring the fetid smell that rose when it was uncovered.

At the bottom of the pit a woman, more girl than

mature, was lying. She wore a knee-length dress of thin white cotton that outlined her shrunken body, and her extended arms and sprawled legs were as thin as young tree-branches. Her face was turned upward, her eyes closed, and her fragile form stirred only as she breathed. Jessie could not repress the exclamation of shock that burst from her lips when she saw that the woman's head looked like a skull, so deeply indrawn were her cheeks and lips.

"Hurry, Ki!" Jessie exclaimed.

Ki was already levering himself into the pit. He lifted the woman and stood with her in his arms while Jessie hurriedly cleared away the brush on one side. Then he laid his light burden on the ground and levered himself out of the excavation to join Jessie, who was on her knees now, bending forward, her fingers clasped on one of the recumbent woman's wrists.

"Her pulse isn't strong, but it's regular," Jessie said. "Carry her down to the horses, Ki. She needs food at once, and it'll be easier and quicker to take her where it is than to bring it up here."

Ki bent down and cradled the woman in his arms. She was such a light burden that he had no difficulty in rising to his feet with her in his arms.

"She doesn't weigh more than fifty or sixty pounds," he told Jessie as he started toward the horses. "It's a wonder that she's still alive, if she's been here since the killings."

"I'm sure she has," Jessie said as she moved up to walk beside Ki. She reached out and put her fingers on the woman's wrist. After a moment she went on, "Her pulse is surprisingly regular. It's not normal, but it's not fluttery, either."

"We'll have to feed her very carefully, though," Ki cautioned. "There's no way of knowing how long she's been without food, but I'd say she's been hiding out here since the other Orientals were killed, and that was more than two months ago."

"I'm sure you're right," Jessie agreed as they reached the horses. "Hold her for just a minute more while I get my bedroll free and spread it for her to lie on."

Jessie made quick work of spreading her bedroll, and Ki laid the fragile form of the woman or girl, he hadn't yet been able to make a guess at her age, on the blanket.

"What can we give her to eat?" he asked Jessie. "She's been starving for such a long time that she can't have any solid food for a while, and all we've got is crackers and jerky."

"Don't worry," Jessie told him. "I've been carrying one of Mr. Borden's milk airtights in my saddlebag for the last three or four months, and I can't seem to remember to take it out. Milk is the best thing she can have now. If you'll get me a canteen, I'll mix a little of it in my travel cup with some water."

Jessie had punctured small holes in the top of the condensed milk can by the time Ki returned with the canteen. She took out her folding travel cup and filled it half-full of water, added the thick condensed milk and swished the cup a few times to blend the liquids.

"Before we can give her this we'll have to revive

her, or wake her up if she's just fallen asleep," Jessie frowned. "Try rubbing her wrists and arms while I wet my handkerchief and rub it on her face."

A few moments after Jessie and Ki had started their ministrations, the woman's eyelids fluttered and opened. She blinked her almond lids a time or two, her dark eyes seeming overlarge in her shrunken face as she gazed up at Jessie, who was bending over her watching anxiously for the signs of her revival. She tried to say something, but only a few weak garbled noises came from her lips.

"Don't try to talk," Jessie told her. "Just sip this milk when I hold it for you."

Slipping an arm behind the woman's shoulders, Jessie lifted her almost weightless torso until she was in a semi sitting posture, then with her free hand took the milk from Ki and tilted it to the woman's lips. After a few futile efforts to control them, her lips parted and she took a swallow of the rich liquid. She gulped and choked as she swallowed, but managed to let the milk flow down her throat.

"We'll have to be careful not to give her too much," Ki cautioned. "There's no way of knowing how long it's been since she's had anything to eat or drink. If she gets even a tiny bit too much in her stomach—"

"Yes, I know," Jessie said. "I'm being very careful, Ki. I'll let her have one more sip, because she needs to begin rebuilding her strength. Then in about five minutes she can drink a little more. We'll see how she is then."

For the next hour, Jessie and Ki hovered anxiously over the girl. Jessie gave her scanty swallows of the rich milk two or three times, and with each sip the fragile woman grew more alert and gained strength. Twice she fell asleep, but each time her eyes closed and her fragile body relaxed she woke with a moaning cry, her thin arms and legs twitching.

During the moments when their new charge wakened, they could see signs of her returning strength. After she'd had perhaps a dozen sips of the milk her intervals of sleep grew shorter and the time she could stay awake lengthened. The afternoon was well along before her eyes stayed open after swallowing a half-dozen spoonfuls of the rich restorative milk, and she looked from Jessie to Ki with genuine awareness in her eyes. Then she spoke a few words of singsong Chinese in a small whispering, questioning voice.

"Can you understand what she said, Ki?" Jessie asked with a puzzled frown.

"Yes, she's talking *pia-hua*. It's a sort of bridging dialect in China. It's a blend of Mandarin and Cantonese and two or three of the other variations of their languages. She asked who we are. I won't tell her anything but our names. If I say anything else, it will only confuse her more."

"Did you get her name?"

"Yes. She is Moy-Tae-On. Now I will tell her to rest and sleep. She has had food, that was what she needed most."

Ki turned to the woman and though he said fewer than a dozen words, the worried frown faded from her face. Then she closed her eyes and fell asleep again. Jessie lowered her frail shoulders to the blanket and looked up at Ki.

"What did you tell her?" she asked.

"To sleep and not to worry, that we were friends, and that we'll look after her. She's still too weak to do anything but nod that she understood."

"How in the world could she have survived such a long time?" Jessie frowned. "Alone, in a deserted place like this?"

"Perhaps because she was alone," Ki suggested. "Those miners must've had some food stored away. The river's close, so she didn't lack for water."

"I suppose that's right," Jessie agreed. "It's lucky we came along when we did, though. She wouldn't've survived very much longer. But now we can get the real story of what happened here from someone who saw it all, and who'd have no reason to tell us anything but the truth."

"I do not like to think of that day," Moy-Tae-On told Jessie and Ki.

She sank back on the blanket, closed her eyes and shook her head. They remained silent, waiting for her to go on. After a moment she opened her eyes and looked at them.

During the remainder of the previous day, through the long night, and until now, when the second day was drawing to a close, Jessie and Ki had kept a constant vigil beside her, one of them awake at all times while the other slept.

Each time the girl had awakened from her restless sleep and opened her eyes, they'd given her more of the rich condensed milk diluted with water.

Though she could not yet stand without assistance or walk without being supported, she'd made a remarkable recovery. Now she could speak, though her words came slowly. Her voice was still barely more than a whisper, and there were times when it faded and failed.

Jessie and Ki had been totally surprised when Moy-Tae-On first spoke to them in English. They had not yet found out how or where she'd learned the language. She had been able only to confirm the fact that she was the only one of the group of Orientals who'd survived the massacre.

Even now, they had not yet learned how she'd managed to escape the bullets that had wiped out the others or how she had managed to survive alone in Hell's Canyon during the weeks that had passed since the senseless killings.

Now Ki urged, "You must tell us what happened here, Moy-Tae-On, even if it is painful to remember. Take all the time you need, and stop talking when you are tired."

"I will try," Moy-Tae-On replied. "But I do not know of everything that happened."

"First tell us how many of you there were," Jessie suggested. "We've heard so many different stories that we're not sure about much of anything."

"We were thirty-two. No, thirty-three," she answered. "A baby was born here."

"How many men and how many women?" Ki asked.

"Seven women."

"I heard that there were some Japanese in your group," Ki went on. "Is that true?"

Moy-Tae-On nodded, a weak lowering of her head that was almost imperceptible, then she said, "Yes. But only four."

"Three of them were of my family," Ki told her. His voice was very sober.

"I did not know much of them," Moy-Tae-On said. "But they are dead with all the others."

"Yes. I was sure they would be." Ki's voice was flat and his face expressionless. He went on, "I did not mean to break into your story. Please, tell us more."

"There is not much to tell, and it hurts me to think about what was done," Moy-Tae-On said. "But I am trying."

She paused for a moment, sipping again from the cup of milk that Jessie had placed beside the blanket. Then she went on, "My parents knew I could not find a husband in our village, so I came here with my father. He saved each yuan he earned for many years to pay our ship-fare, but he was sure he could find a man to marry me. He thought we would find much gold in a little time, and a rich woman finds a husband faster than one who has nothing. This is why I studied to speak the English."

When Moy-Tae-On paused for breath again, Jessie broke in, "You have very little strength right now, Moy-Tae-On. Please don't waste it telling us about things that happened before the killers came here. We can learn about them later."

"Jessie's right," Ki nodded. "You and the others came here looking for gold, and I'm sure you must've found some. That must've been what the men who shot your friends were after."

"We learned that the gold was not as we had thought it was," the Chinese girl replied.

"You didn't find any?" Jessie frowned.

"We found gold, but it was not as we had been told. It was in tiny pieces almost too small to see. Some were not as big even as a grain of sand."

"That's what's called flake gold," Ki told her.

"This word we learned," Moy-Tae-On nodded. "And we learned as well that it is very hard work to get much."

"But you managed to save some, I'm sure," Ki said.

"Of course, but first we dig on land a long time. Then we see gold in the river. We swim, dive, get sand in hand, and maybe sometimes is gold with sand.".

"You panned the gold with your bare hands?" Jessie asked incredulously.

"Not enough of us have pans," Moy-Tae-On shrugged.

"Then the only gold you found was in the river?" Jessie went on.

Moy-Tae-On nodded, "Only in river was gold. We sleep in holes we dig looking for gold when nights get cold."

"And what happened to the gold?" Ki asked. "Did the men who attacked you get it?"

"This I am not know, Ki."

"Do you know how many sacks of gold there were?" Jessie asked.

"Many. How many, I do not know."

"Then the men who did the killing didn't find it?" Ki was frowning when he asked the question.

"They find it. Not all when killing, they look then, but not find all. Then they come back."

"They came here a second time?" Jessie frowned.

Moy-Tae-On nodded. "After one day, maybe two. I do not remember some things so good. I am afraid. I hide. I have no food. I go look at dead ones, not find any alive. Then I go hide again."

"But you were here when they came back?" Ki asked her.

"Yes. But in trees, hiding. After they leave, I come out."

"How long was it before they came the second time?"

"One day, Ki. Maybe two. I am not sure. I have no food, I sleep much."

"And they searched all around that time?" Jessie asked.

"Yes. They throw all dead in river. Look for gold then."

"And they didn't see you?" Jessie asked quickly.

"I hide first time, go far in woods. Not so far not see them shooting. Was very bad."

"How many men were there?" Ki asked.

"Six, eight. Some do not come this side river, they stand on bank across, shoot with long guns."

"Rifles?" Jessie prompted.

"Yes," Moy-Tae-On nodded. "Men this side use long guns, little guns, too. Kill men in water. Kill men on bank. Kill all but me."

A puzzled frown had grown on Jessie's face while she and Ki were questioning Moy-Tae-On. Now she asked, "You said they came back a day or two later?

Is that when they looked for the gold you and the others had gotten from the river?"

Moy-Tae-On shook her head. "Yes. And they find gold first time too. Look a long time, I stay in woods but come close to see when no more shooting. Hear them talk."

"Do you remember anything they said?" Jessie asked.

"They talk about not that they want to come back. But they take dead men from shore, put them in river."

"Did you hear them call any names while they talked?" Ki asked.

"Names?" Moy-Tae-On frowned.

"Their names," Ki persisted. "If you heard them talking they must have used names."

"Maybe they didn't, Ki," Jessie broke in. "From what Moy-Tae-On has said, I think she has a very vivid memory. She'd have remembered the names of the men if she'd heard them. And we've encountered enough outlaws to know that they're usually pretty careful just to use nicknames or even false names, when they're talking to one another during a holdup."

"But I want the names of those outlaws, Jessie!" Ki's usually calm voice was angry now. "They killed people of my family! I want to know who they are so I can hunt them down!" He turned back to Moy-Tae-On. "Are you sure you don't remember hearing any names?"

Moy-Tae-On shook her head. "I do not remember, Ki. I am very much afraid when I hear them come back. I go as far from river to hide as can before they see me. When they stop and throw dead ones in river, I am stay where I hide."

"And you watched them throw your friends' bodies in the river?" Jessie asked.

"Yes. I stay still like small mouse. I am think they find me and kill me, too."

"You'd know these men again if you saw them, I suppose?" Ki asked. His voice was level again, but Jessie knew him well enough to realize how much effort it took to keep his anger from spilling out.

"I am not ever to forget them, Ki." Moy-Tae-On's voice was thin and fading now.

"Please Ki," Jessie broke in. "Put off your questions until later, when Moy-Tae-On is stronger. We know where the killers are. They're at the Locked O's."

"I haven't forgotten, Jessie."

"Neither of us have, or will," Jessie assured him. "But we've got an entirely new set of problems now, Ki. We'd better be solving them before we make any further plans."

"Moy-Tae-On?" Ki asked.

"Yes. And food. We didn't plan to stay here, so we didn't bring a lot with us. But I think there's an answer, Lily and the ferryman must keep some food in reserve. I'm sure we can persuade them to sell us enough to tide us over."

"Then let's start back in the morning," Ki said. "Lily ought to be able to look after Moy-Tae-On while we're gone, too."

"That's also occurred to me," Jessie nodded. "And there's nothing to keep us here. We'll take turns carrying Moy-Tae-On. I think she'll be strong enough to ride by morning."

"Then you and I will go back to the Locked O's," Ki said. "And this time we'll know what to expect. I'm sure it's going to be a different kind of visit from our first one, Jessie!"

★

# Chapter 9

"Of course I'll look after the pore little thing!" Lily exclaimed. Jessie had explained why they needed a place of safety and care where Moy-Tae-On could stay for a few days. "I don't care if she's a Chinee. Why, she ain't nothing but skin and bones! She looks like she's had a real rough time. But I'll get her plumped up and strong again, and be glad to have her company."

"Of course, I'll pay you for her food and pay whatever you think is right for taking care of her," Jessie offered.

"You will up a pig's"—Lily stopped short and re-started—"in a pig's eye! I'll be glad to look after the poor wizened-up little thing. And don't talk about paying me. I ain't running into hard times yet, Jessie. I got plenty of grub tucked away. In a place like this you learn to be ready for bad winters and hard times."

"You wouldn't mind selling us some of that extra food, I hope?" Ki asked. "Judging by what you just said, you've got enough to spare."

"More'n enough. Airtights full of milk and tomatoes and maybe a dozen strings of cured sausage and two hams and dear knows how many sides of bacon and . . . well, we can go in the pantry, and you take however much you figure to need."

"I don't think we'll be gone more than two days," Jessie told Lily. "Ki and I have a little bit of unfinished business that we're going to take care of."

Lily asked no questions but for a moment she looked piercingly at Jessie with her eyes puckered shrewdly. Then she said, "Maybe you and me better step into the pantry, and you see what strikes your fancy to take along."

"Why, all we'll need—" Jessie began before she caught the look on Lily's face, and changed what she'd had mind to say. Instead she nodded and went on, "That sounds like a good idea. Show me the way."

Lily led Jessie into the kitchen and opened the door to a small closetlike lean-to. Her voice dropped, and she said, "I ain't one to talk about my neighbors, Jessie. But if I was to make a guess, you'd say whether I was right or wrong."

"Of course," Jessie agreed.

"Now my guess is that you and Ki's going to be heading south along the river on the other side, maybe for about a day's ride?"

"Yes. My map shows that it's the shortest way to go."

"I didn't ask you no questions about where you're going, and I don't aim to. If push was to come to shove, I wouldn't want to know," Lily went on quickly. "But I can figure as good as the next one."

"I'm sure you can."

"Now, I'm going to say something that might be outa turn. If I had some private business on the other side of the river, I'd shy away from the ferry."

"I'm sure you have good reasons for your suggestion, Lily," Jessie frowned. "But I'll admit I'm curious why you made it."

"I've got to live here, Jessie," Lily replied. "And even if my closest neighbors don't exactly live next door, I need to get along with 'em, ain't that right?"

"Why of course."

"Now, Frank Smith wouldn't likely be running the ferry if he was an outlaw, but he's sure friendly with some of the men that are. It wasn't long before you and Ki and that little Chinee girl got here when two of Frank's friends went past on the way to the ferry. I knew 'em from before, so they pulled up long enough for us to say howdy. They said they was figuring to stop and visit with him for a day or two before they pushed on south to start work at the Locked O's."

"I think I understand, what you're driving at," Jessie nodded, remembering the stir that she and Ki had raised at the ranch. "And thank you for warning us. But I don't see any way to avoid the ferry

119

crossing. We're going to be taking the road south on the other side of the river."

"That ain't nothing to worry about. All you and Ki's got to do is take the trail on this side of the canyon and ride down to Pittsburg Landing. You can wade your horses across the Snake there. It won't be all that much out of your way."

After a moment of thoughtful silence Jessie nodded and said, "You know the country and the people around here a lot better than Ki and I do, Lily. If that's your advice, we'd be foolish not to follow it."

"You won't be sorry for doing it," Lily assured her. "Now. Let's you and me step into this pantry here and you pick out what you figure you'll need to keep you going for a few days."

"It's just as well that we are going along the west bank of the river," Ki told Jessie. They were passing the point where the forbidding black basalt ledges began rising between the trail and the river. He went on, "We were in such a hurry to take Moy-Tae-On where she could get the kind of food she needed that we just looked over that Chinese camp hit-or-miss. There might be another survivor who found a safe place to hide."

"I sympathize with your feelings about your relatives, Ki," Jessie said. "But from what Lily told us about the shootings and how the killers got rid of the bodies, I'm sure you know that there's no possibility at all of anyone else being alive."

"Common sense tells me the same thing, Jessie.

But in spite of what we know, I can't convince myself to give up hope."

"We'll stop and take another look at the place where the Orientals were panning for gold, then. But I'm sure we won't find anybody else alive."

They rode on in companionable silence as the quiet whisper of the Snake rose in volume and the character of the river began to change. Its bubbling surface became a frothy torrent that gave a somber hint of the currents and crosscurrents and undertows that could swallow a tangle of floating brush or a man or a horse with equal ease.

As Jessie and Ki rode further upstream the very water began to change color. It was no longer green-grey, but a dark forbidding hue that was almost as black as the cliffs. Its low ripples rose in volume in the places where it growled in froth-covered waves and created small snarling echoes between the high somberly black walls of stone that formed its banks.

"That river looks even more unfriendly now than it did the first time we saw it, Ki," Jessie remarked, breaking a long period of silence. "I'll be glad when we get to the wide spot where it spreads out."

"We've still got a good stretch to cover," Ki reminded her. "But we'll be well on our way to reaching Pittsburg Landing when we pass the place where the Orientals were camped."

"I haven't forgotten what you said a while ago, that you want to stop for another look there. I hope you won't be too disappointed if we don't find much of anything, though. It seemed to me that the men who killed the Orientals cleaned out their camp pretty thoroughly."

"They did, Jessie. But all those people who were killed have relatives who'll be worrying if they don't hear from the emigrants. And a list of their names might be hidden where they were camping."

"It's possible, of course," Jessie agreed. "We didn't have time to make a really thorough search of all those bed-shelters, we were too concerned about Moy-Tae-On. Which reminds me, Ki. Surely she'd know the names of everyone who was there."

"I'm not thinking of the names of the people who were there, but their relatives," Ki told her. "You know how much importance we Orientals place on family."

"Yes, of course. And perhaps we'll have good luck. With both of us looking and knowing the lay of the land, it won't take us too long to make a pretty thorough search."

They pushed steadily ahead until they reached the spot where the river widened. Here the constant roiling roar of its swift current faded, and the black stone ridges that confined the river and formed its banks slanted gradually downward into the sandy soil until they vanished underground.

Both Jessie and Ki were familiar with their surroundings now. They dismounted at the edge of the flat, and after tethering their horses at the edge of a clump of brush they began walking along the bank. They reached the center of the area where the bed-shelters were located and stopped to look from the river's edge to the expanse of brush-studded ground that led back to the trees. Here and there a clump of dry twigs and brittle bleached weeds marked the location of one of the bed-shelters.

"Suppose you start at this side of the clearing," Ki suggested. "I'll go on to the other edge, and we'll work back and forth from the river and meet somewhere near the center."

"It's as good a way as any," Jessie nodded. "As long as we're searching, let's do a thorough job."

They separated and started searching, moving from one to another of the clumps of dry brush and scraps of bedding-rags that marked the location of the small rectangular excavations. After Jessie had looked into the first two or three she was struck by their sameness and the evidence of the poverty that they provided.

It was obvious to her that after the men who'd shot the Orientals finished their merciless work and began searching the encampment for gold they'd explored the bed-pits and from most of them had lifted out the scraps of rags that had been used for bedding. During the time that had passed since the cold-blooded murders the elements had been at work. Winds had scattered the scraps, and at some time a heavy rain had beaten them into the earth. The pieces of cloth were almost invisible, covered as they were by a thin film of the fine-grained, sandy, ocher soil.

In most of the holes where the bed-scraps remained they'd also been beaten into the earth by the rain, and like those on the surface, the dusty soil had formed a fragile crust over the bits and pieces of fabric. To save herself from having to kneel and grope in the bottom of the bed-pits, Jessie had picked up a long sturdy branch to use as prod in exploring the pits.

She'd prodded into a half-dozen of the small excavations without discovering anything except the pitiful bed-rags when the dry branch she was using snapped and broke as she began lifting the crusted rags from the hole. They dropped back to the bottom, and when Jessie peered into the little rectangular pit, she saw a small buckskin pouch lying exposed.

Jessie had seen too many like it to fail to recognize it. She stood up and looked for Ki. He was halfway across the clearing, bending down into one of the bed-pits.

"Ki!" she called. "Come over here for a minute! I'm sure I've found a poke full of gold!"

Ki wasted no time. He started toward her, and Jessie dropped to her knees beside the pouch. She stretched to reach it, finally closed her hand over it and was just getting to her feet when Ki reached her side. She held out the plump leather pouch for him to see before she started picking at the knot on the drawstring.

"It looks like a gold poke," Ki agreed.

"And it's heavy enough to be one, too."

Jessie finally managed to loosen the knot of the stiff thong and pulled the pouch mouth open. In the bright sunlight the gleam of gold was unmistakable.

"It is gold, Ki!" Jessie exclaimed.

"Yes. Very fine gold, even finer than seems possible."

Ki touched the tip of his forefinger to his tongue and poked the finger into the glittering dust. When he lifted his arm and the sunlight touched the tiny flakes, they glowed with the dull but unmistakable lustre of raw gold.

"How tiny those grains are!" Jessie exclaimed. "Why, they look even smaller than the grains of sand on the riverbottom!"

"They are smaller. Flake dust is always this small, Jessie. Men who've worked in the placer diggings have told me that. But they say it's gold in purest form, so fine that it doesn't need to be run through a smelter to take out impurities."

"It's not any more valuable, though," Jessie frowned. "I see gold quotations when I have a chance to go into a big bank or stockbroker's office in one of the cities we visit. I've never seen anything like 'flake gold' listed."

"No. But weight for weight, it has the same value." Ki took the pouch from Jessie and hefted it while he very carefully scraped the bit of gold dust off his fingertip and allowed it to shower down into the poke.

"How much would you guess that poke weighs, Ki?" Jessie asked. "If I remember the figures on the stockmarket page of the last newspaper I looked at before we left San Francisco, the Mining Exchange was posting six dollars an ounce for gold."

Ki was silent for a moment as he hefted the poke and did some mental arithmetic. He said, "I can't guess to an ounce how much this poke weighs, but I'd guess there's something like seven or eight hundred dollars worth in it."

"That's a lot of money to an Oriental gold panner," Jessie told him. "And we don't have any idea how many pokes like this the men who killed these people stole."

"There's more to it than that," Ki said soberly. "Those Orientals weren't working as hard as they did just for the gold they panned, Jessie. It was the key that would open a door for their start here in America."

"It was a lot of money for the murdering thieves who killed them for it," Jessie put in, her voice angry.

"We'll have to look in all the other bed-holes, the ones we haven't checked yet," Ki said. "I don't suppose we'll find any more bags of gold. I'm sure the men who killed those people must've found any pokes that were in their beds, like this one."

"I don't suppose they'd have hidden any someplace besides their bed-holes," Jessie said, shaking her head.

"They might have," Ki frowned. "If they did, it'll probably never be found. There are hundreds of places within ten or fifteen steps from here where they could've hidden something as small as a gold poke."

"Of course," Jessie agreed, looking at the untouched wilderness around them. "Under one of those boulders along the riverbed, in the crotch of a tree, maybe even in a hole in the ground marked by some sign nobody else would recognize. If they did hide any more pokes, it'd just be an accident if we happened to find one."

"Instead of wasting time looking for something that might not even be here, we'd better be pushing on to the Locked O's," Ki said. "There is no hope I will find anything here to tell me what might have happened to my relatives."

"I'm sorry to have to say this, Ki, but you're right," Jessie nodded. "If we move right along, we should be getting there just before daybreak. I can't think of a better time to take those killers by surprise."

They started walking back toward their horses, angling across the little clearing to the spot where the animals were tethered. A hundred yards still separated them from their mounts when a rifle's sharp crack sounded above the soft sussurus of the river. A bullet whizzed past Jessie's head.

It missed by only a few inches, and both she and Ki dropped flat as a second shot followed the first. Jessie had whipped out her Colt while she was diving to the ground. She raised her head to find a target and saw two men on horseback on the opposite side of the river. Both held their rifles shouldered.

Jessie saw at a glance that the riders were beyond the range of her Colt and did not answer their fire. She looked at Ki, who was stretched flat on the barren earth a few feet away from her. His eyes were fixed on the riders just as hers had been a few seconds earlier.

A short distance behind Ki, Jessie also saw the small pile of brush that one of them had pulled from an abandoned bed-pit when they were examining the sleeping-places a bit earlier. The crack of a rifle from one of the riders on the river's eastern bank broke the stillness again. Neither Jessie nor Ki presented an easy target now. The rifle-bullet kicked up a spurt of fine sand between them.

"Bed-shelter, Ki! It's just behind us!" Jessie said. "We can both get in it if we squeeze a little bit."

"You get in it fast and wait," Ki told her. "I'm going after my rifle!"

Jessie began crawfish-crawling along the ground toward the little brush-heap. During the two or three minutes required for her to reach the heap of brush and drop into the bed-pit she'd kept her attention focused on the riders across the river.

Kneeling on the bottom of the cramped shallow pit, she raised her head above the edge. This time she located their attackers after only a moment of looking. They were rising in their stirrups, their heads swiveling as they looked for their targets who had vanished so suddenly.

Jessie had also lost sight of Ki. She glanced at the spot where he'd been when she saw him last, then moved her eyes past it in the direction of their horses. A vague flicker of movement caught her attention a half-dozen paces beyond Ki's earlier position, and Jessie realized that it was Ki on his way to get the rifle from its saddle-scabbard on his horse.

Though Jessie had seen Ki move *ninja*-style many times, she still had trouble following him as he snaked along the ground in the direction of his tethered horse. Even now, when she knew the direction in which he was heading, she could get only the suggestion of a bit of motion now and then, a flicker of some half-suggested shape, the quick ripple of a patch darker than the ground. It was not until Ki levered himself up to pull his rifle out of its saddle scabbard that she got a recognizable glimpse, and then it lasted no more than two or three seconds.

Although time had seemed to stand still during the interval between the first two shots from across the river and the three or four that had followed while Jessie and Ki were still exposed to the snipers, only a few minutes had actually elapsed. The snipers were still sitting in their saddles, rifles ready in their hands and looking for targets, at the time when Ki reached his horse.

"Where the hell did them two go?" one of the riders called to his companion.

"Damned if I know!" the other man said. "I know for sure that I seen 'em before we reined in, then all of a sudden they wasn't there."

"They can't be far," the man who'd spoken first went on. "There's the heads of their nags poking up over that little stand of brush just downriver from that clearing where we taken care of them Chinks."

"We'll wait and get 'em when they show again. They're damn sure still over there."

By this time Ki had wormed and wriggled *ninja*-style back to the bed-pit where Jessie had taken cover. He stopped behind the fringe of grasses and weeds that gave him a semblance of shelter and dropped his voice to a loud whisper.

"Just stay where you are, Jessie. We don't have anything to worry about."

"I'm not worrying, Ki. I just wish they'd go about their business so we can finish ours."

"They'll move on in a minute," Ki assured her. "They're from that outlaw gang at the Locked O's, all right. But the river's between us, so we don't have too much to worry about."

"I'm not worrying, Ki. I'm sure they were just sent here to find out whether anybody's been prowling around. All we have to do is stay holed up until they move along. Then it'll be safe to go about our own business."

★

# Chapter 10

The riders on the other side of the river resumed their conversation.

"Right now I'd a long sight sooner know what them outlanders are doing here than worry about where they've gone to cover," the first man went on. "Hell and damnation! We done that job on them Chinks more'n two months ago, and now them two shows up and starts nosing around like they're onto something."

"They can't be! There wasn't a Chink left alive when we'd finished!" his companion said.

"Maybe we missed seeing some that had hid out."

"Not likely, Stilts. Remember, Plub sworn up and down and sideways that nobody'd ever miss them damn Chinks or come here looking for 'em, once we'd got rid of 'em."

"Damn it, Bittman! You think I don't remember?" Stilts asked. "It'll be a long time before I forget what he said, let alone what we done that day."

"You sound like you're getting soft. And Plub won't like that one little bit."

"Soft, hell! Call it careful. That'd be more like it."

"Maybe," Bittman said. "Now cut out your palaver. The only thing on my mind right now is to get whoever it is poking around on the other side of the river. I got a notion if Plub was here he'd send us over there to look. All we know now is there's two of 'em. We better go across and see what else we can find out."

"Ride all the way down to Pittsburg Landing and then all the way back? Why, that's gonna take us the rest of the day! I halfway figured we'd be back to the ranch in time for supper."

"I didn't say nothing about Pittsburg Landing," Bittman told Stilts. "But I forgot you ain't in on it yet. I guess Plub's made up his mind you'll do to ride with."

"Maybe you better tell me what you're getting at," Stilts suggested.

"We don't have to go all the way upstream to Pittsburg Landing to get to the other side of the river. We can cross right here on this flat stretch."

"You got to be joshing me, Bittman! All I ever heard about the Snake since I got here from Wyoming is that there's no place you can cross it in Hell's Canyon."

"Sure. That's what you heard. That's what Plub and the boss that run things before he was taken over wants everybody to think," Bittman explained. "Now, say you're on the run, headed for the Locked O's to hide out. You cross here and you're safe at the ranch and whoever's after you swings downriver to Joseph's Crossing or upstream to Pittsburg Landing."

"I guess I'd beat 'em to the Locked O's," Stilts said.

"You damn sure would," Bittman agreed. "And be tucked away where they couldn't find you. Now, just keep in mind what I've told you and don't let on you know about this place."

"Don't worry. I ain't aiming to get Plub mad at me again. He like to taken the skin offen me the other night when we let that Chink get away."

"All right," Bittman went on. "Now you only got two things to watch for. It's a pretty easy scrabble on both sides close to shore where the bottom's loose sand. But there's a fast current right in the middle, the water's deep there."

"How deep? And how wide?"

"Nobody's ever fell in and hit bottom and come out alive," Bittman told him. "But there's maybe twenty or thirty feet in the middle where the current's right wild." As he was speaking, he disengaged one foot from its stirrup and bent his leg up to slip his boot off.

"What the hell you doing?" Stilts asked.

"That's a fool question if I ever heard one. You

got eyes, ain't you? Can't you see I'm taking off my boots so I don't get 'em full of water?"

"I guess I better do the same thing, then."

"I guess," Bittman said. He was taking the boot off his other foot as he talked. "Remember to keep your nag's head upstream. Now get them boots off in a hurry and tie 'em on like I am, so they won't fill up so bad."

For a moment the two outlaws were silent, fixing their boots in place. At last Bittman asked, "You got it all straight now about what to do?"

"It ain't a hell of a lot to remember, and I don't forget things like that," Stilts replied.

"Come on, then. We'll cross on over there and get rid of whoever them two is prowling around."

Jessie and Ki watched the two outlaws closely as they toed their horses to the riverbank and started down its steep sides to the water's edge. When their riders reined in to survey the stream and then reached behind their saddles and slapped the animals on their rumps to urge them into the water, the horses began jerking their heads up and loosing strings of high-pitched protesting whinnies.

Bittman and Stilts had slipped their feet out of their stirrups and were holding their legs high, stretched forward, in anticipation of the moment when they'd enter the deeper water. The horses were tamer now, and finally began moving forward.

Jessie said to Ki, "We'll wait until they get in the deep channel, and then cut loose. I don't have any compunction at all about shooting first."

"I'll fire when you do, then," Ki told her.

Jessie nodded and they settled back to wait.

From the bank almost to the center of the river the animals moved slowly and steadily until they were chest-deep into the river. Bittman's horse lurched forward and loosed a string of high-pitched protesting whinnies when its front hooves reached the center channel and dropped into the deep water. The outlaw used the loose ends of his gathered reins to lash the animal's neck three or four times, and it steadied down.

While crossing the center channel the horse held its head high as it churned through the swift current it encountered in the deep, fast-flowing water. The river carried it a dozen or more yards downstream in spite of its efforts to obey the reins as Bittman hauled on them trying to keep on a straight course.

Stilts was having more trouble than Bittman. His horse was refusing to buck the deep swift midstream current. It persisted in trying to turn downriver in spite of all the commands he shouted and did not respond to his persistent yanking on the reins.

Bittman's mount reared up as its forefeet touched bottom again. It reared upward and heaved and churned the water until all four feet were planted on the bottom in the shallows beyond the channel. Then it took a few more steps and stopped where the water rose only to its hocks.

Stilts was still in the grip of the current. Bittman looked back and saw his companion's predicament. He pulled his lariat free of the saddle string and worked it into a small loop. With a warning shout he tossed the loop to Stilts, who managed to grab the lariat and drop the loop around his saddle-horn.

Bittman's horse was still standing up to its hock-joints in the water and had not yet been able to plant its feet solidly on dry ground. Instead of serving as a safe anchor, Stilts's horse tried to turn while still belly-deep at the edge of the Snake's heavy midstream current. Now the merciless river took command. The drag of the lariat began forcing Bittman's horse downstream.

Though Bittman's horse tried to turn, it was dragged back. Now it stood belly-deep in the slack water, only a few feet from the river's swift midstream raceway. Twenty or thirty feet separated it from the dry ground beyond the shallows. The drag of the lariat holding Stilts was too great. The irresistible current forced the animal back into the river. The threshing of its legs as it fought the heavy flow got its forefeet tangled in the lariat.

Bittman was trying to keep himself in the saddle in spite of his horse's gyrations. All the time the icy chill of the water was sapping the strength of both men and horses. Their struggles became more and more feeble as they were tossed and turned in the turbulent river.

Jessie and Ki stood watching the outlaws struggling in the current. Jessie was holding her rifle ready, but had not yet shouldered it. Ki looked at her questioningly.

"We'd be fools to try to ride out and rescue them," she replied to his unspoken question. "Even if we wanted to, we'd be in the same fix they are in that current. But we can toss them a rope if they toss their guns in the water."

Ki lowered his rifle. "All we can do is offer. But

even if we do, I doubt they'll be smart enough to take it."

Raising her voice, wondering if the outlaws would be able to hear her over the constant roar of the rushing current, she called, "You men out there! Toss your guns in the river and put your hands over your heads!"

Jessie need not have worried about her shout reaching the outlaws' ears. Both Bittman and Stilts turned at the sound of her voice, both dropping their hands to their hip holsters to draw. The horses felt their reins go slack and stopped struggling against the Snake's powerful current. They let it carry them along the line of least resistance, downstream.

Belatedly, the outlaws realized their mistake. Without releasing their weapons they grabbed for the reins, but their efforts were too late. Stilts, riding upstream from Bittman, was the first to lose control of his horse. Confused at having no pressure on the reins to guide it, the animal surrendered to the current that was pushing it. The force of the wild river's eddying currents whirled the horse in midriver and began to push horse and rider downstream.

Bittman saw his danger too late. He grabbed for the reins without dropping his revolver, but one hand on the leathers was not enough. The horse threshed for only a moment before Stilts and his mount crashed into it.

Neither Bittman nor Stilts had time to brace themselves before the midstream collision of their mounts. Their arms flailed the air as they fought to stay in their saddles, but it was a doomed effort. The current was carrying them ever-faster, their horses were threshing, trying to buck off the riders, and only a few swift seconds passed before the current took command.

Bittman went under first, then as Stilts fought in a vain effort to grab his companion, he, too, lost the battle to the river. Both men were quite literally dragged from their saddles by the river's fast heavy flow. Without the burden of their riders, the horses had strength enough to resume their frantic swim toward the shore. Both animals churned and bobbed as they fought the drag of the Snake's currents and made their way to shore.

With the loss of their horses, the outlaws also lost any chance they might have had to survive. Their clothing was wet now, and its weight combined with the current's powerful drag was too much for them to sustain.

Stilts' arms churned the water as he tried to reach Bittman, but before he could cover even a fraction of the distance that separated them Bittman's head vanished below the surface. Stilts made a feeble effort to turn and head toward shore, but before he'd splashed two strokes the Snake claimed him just as easily as it had swallowed his companion. Now only the heads and necks of the horses swimming toward the bank broke the surface of the swift roiling river.

Standing on the bank, Jessie and Ki had watched their enemies lose their brief struggle with the Snake. Two to three minutes had been enough for the treacherous powerful stream to claim its victims.

"I don't like to watch anybody die that way, even

our enemies," Jessie said soberly as she turned to Ki.

"It's not a pleasant thing to look at," he agreed. "But the river certainly solved our problems for us."

"Not completely," Jessie reminded him. "We've still got the rest of the gang to deal with."

"I'm not overlooking that, Jessie. But without the pair that the Snake River just swallowed, they're going to be two men short."

"Only until the two that stopped to visit the ferryman at Joseph's Crossing get to the ranch," Jessie pointed out.

"We've faced bigger gangs before," Ki shrugged. "And if we cross here right now, we'll get to the Locked O's about the time the outlaws will be bedding down for the night."

"It's still a ride to Pittsburg Landing. We're only halfway there. And once we're on the other side of the river, we'll have to backtrack to the ranch. By the time we get there, it'll be full daylight." Jessie was studying the river as she spoke. "But now that we know we can cross the river here . . ."

"My guess is that there's just one short stretch to the bottle-neck that must be on the bottom," Ki said thoughtfully. "If you think it's worth the risk . . ."

"Yes, I think it is," she replied slowly. "We can cut the risk by riding upstream a little way, Ki. It's easier to angle across a current as heavy as this one must be than it is to try to cut directly across."

"If we've seen all that we need to see here, we might as well start, then."

Jessie had been studying the river, both upstream

and down. She caught sight of one of the horses ridden by the dead outlaws. It was a hundred yards away, nosing for grass at the edge of the clearing.

"Let's catch that horse first," she suggested. "We'll lash our saddlebags on its back and put our rifles on top of the load where they'll be high enough above the water to stay dry."

Ki was starting for his horse while Jessie was still speaking. He walked the animal up to the other horse, leaned low to grab its reins, and led it back to where Jessie was waiting. Together they made a quick job of securing their gear on its back, with their rifles riding high atop the load.

"Boots next, I guess," Ki said. His voice was as emotionless as though he was telling her what hour of the day it was. He levered out of his own boots and gingerly picked his way on the broken earth beside the river's edge to where Jessie sat on her mount. She took off her hand-stitched boots and passed them to him; Ki lashed them with his own beside the rifles that were on top of the horse's load.

"I guess you remember the place where those two men tried to cross," Jessie said after they'd mounted their own horses.

"Of course. I was surprised when they started across, but as soon as I saw what they intended to do I took a good look at the place where they went into the river."

"It's the channel we'll have to swim that I'm thinking of, Ki." Jessie was toeing her horse into motion as she spoke. She reined it upriver along the bank, looking ahead at the wide stream's decept-

140

ively placid surface. She went on, "You saw how fast it swept those two men downstream after they got into it."

"I think that all we have to do is get the horses to a fairly good pace before we reach the channel," Ki told her. "If we don't worry as much about the current as we do about staying on our course, we ought to be all right."

"Do you suppose the Chinese ever got across?" she frowned. "No one can swim in that current."

"As a guess, I'd say they used a rope," Ki frowned. "Two or three of them holding one end on this side of the river. The ones who crossed just let the current carry them to the shallow water on the other side."

"It's too bad we can't cross the same way," Jessie said. "But since we don't have anyone here to hold a rope for us, I guess the only thing to do is swim the horses across."

They were at the widest part of the river now, looking at the clear shallow water lapping the riverbank. They could see the sandy bottom and follow it with their eyes for a dozen yards away from the shore. Beyond that point the current was strong enough to ripple the surface of the water and create patches of foam. The big blobs of tiny moving bubbles not only destroyed their vision, but the glare of the dropping afternoon sun glazed the river's surface with a glaring brilliance that hid the bottom.

Jessie reined her horse into the stream. The thought of Sun, her big palomino so far away at the Circle Star, entered her mind, and she wished that she was astride him instead of a strange livery mount. Then the expanding ring of surface ripples from the hooves of the horse she was actually riding began spreading across the surface of the water directly in front of her. The small rippled wavelets that moved ahead of her and the glare of the sun on the stream hid the river's bottom as effectively as a blindfold.

Behind her, Jessie could hear the soft sussurus made by Ki's mount as it followed her into the shallows. She did not look back, but kept her eyes fixed on the water. It was growing darker as it deepened. In less than a minute, Jessie found that she could no longer see bottom, and she took her eyes off the river to find a landmark on the opposite bank. She picked out a stand of raddled bushes on the far bank, and kept her eyes fixed on them while her horse moved gingerly ahead. The Snake's surface glinted with the glare of the sun. It gave no hint of what lay beneath it.

When a sudden chill swept over her stocking-clad feet, Jessie almost jumped from her saddle in surprise. The start was momentary, for her horse lurched forward then and the chill that had touched her feet so unexpectedly travelled swiftly up the calves of her legs. The icy water stopped climbing there, and the sides of her horse began pulsing as it started to swim.

For the first time, Jessie now felt the full power of the river's rushing current. As her horse breasted the current, the water crawled up its chest to the point of its shoulders and curled into a white-edged line that swept back along its sides. Jessie could feel the animal's muscles tightening as its legs began churning.

Lifting her eyes to glance at the opposite bank, she saw that it was now sliding slowly past her. She slapped her reins on the neck of her mount, but she stopped after two or three thwacks when she realized that the horse was as interested as she was in moving ahead. Through her uncomfortably chilled thighs and calves she could feel the animal's muscles tauten and relax in a steady rhythm as its legs churned underwater.

Glancing ahead at the distant riverbank, Jessie felt a brief moment of something akin to panic when she saw that the bank was sliding past her and that in spite of the horse's efforts the relentless current was slowly carrying them downstream. She did not dare take her eyes off the riverbank that rose beyond a long stretch of the river's more placid shallow surface, and her brow knitted in a worried frown when she saw how fast she and the struggling horse were being carried downstream.

★

# Chapter 11

Suddenly Jessie's horse reared under her, and the rhythm of its legs churning the water gave way to a series of lurches and humpings. Her moment of apprehension ended in a sigh of relief when she realized that the icy waters of the Snake were no longer lapping at her legs. Though her horse still had its hind hooves in the river, and only inches separated her own feet from its waters, the horse's front hooves were now planted firmly on the sandbank and the treacherous currents of the Snake had been defeated.

She leaned forward in the saddle to shift her weight and make it easier for her mount to finish levering up its hind legs and get completely out of the current. It did so with a single strong lunge, and once on the sandy bottom with the swirling currents no longer tugging at it, the horse took an easy stride ahead. Now that she'd defeated the current and was in shallow slack water on a safe stretch of riverbottom, Jessie twisted in her saddle to glance back at Ki.

He was a short distance downstream from her, where the bank was a bit steeper, and his horse was just lifting a front hoof onto the sandbar. Once it found that its footing was on solid ground it pulled itself out of the current quickly, and Ki reined it toward the spot where Jessie sat watching.

"It wasn't as bad as I thought it would be," she called when he'd almost reached her side. Her voice sounded thin in her own ears, which were filled with the steady roar of the river. "Just the same, I'm glad it's over with."

"No more than I am," Ki called back. "But we both know now that it was well worth the risk."

Jessie nodded, her throat was still raspy from the shouting she and Ki had been forced to do. She glanced down at the river's surface. The water was knee-deep to her horse here. Its current was so gentle as to be almost imperceptible, and the water was glass-clear. She could almost count the grains of sand on the bottom. The sand was fine, nearly white, and everywhere Jessie looked she could see the shadowed pocks of a countless number of small shallow craters.

Near two or three of the depressions, dome-shaped circular pans had been shoved edgewise into the sand. From earlier visits to areas where placer mining was carried on, Jessie recognized the utensils as gold-pans. They were shaped to allow the gold-seeker to scoop up a handful of the stream's bottom. When the pan was lifted and tilted slightly, then revolved in a slow circular motion the light sand or earth washed out in tiny dribbles while the heavy flakes of gold that had been mixed with the riverbed sand soil settled to the bottom of the pan.

Jessie pointed to the pans on the bottom to call Ki's attention to them.

"Yes," he nodded. "I saw quite a few just like them downstream in the shallows while I was crossing the sand. Those outlaws must have shot a lot of the people while they were still at work in the river here."

"For some reason that I can't quite explain, it makes me angrier than ever to see what those men did," Jessie told him. Her voice was uncharacteristically hard.

"Outlaws are outlaws wherever they're found," Ki commented. "We've had plenty of proof of that."

"Yes," she agreed, then went on, "Let's don't spend any more time looking backward, Ki. Right now I'm more anxious than ever to get to the Locked O's. Even if we don't have any legal standing, we can march those outlaws from their hideout and into the nearest town where there's any law. Then the authorities can handle things the rest of the way."

"I'm as ready to do that as you are, Jessie. You already know how strongly I feel about what happened here."

Even though the rest given them had been brief, the horses moved willingly as Jessie and Ki rode the rest of the way across the flat sandy bottom, through the calm shallows, and up the sharp incline of the riverbank. The trace of a trail that wound beside the stream was deserted. After retrieving their guns and saddle bags and giving a final backward look at the ill-fated stretch of river they were leaving, they toed their horses to a brisk but muscle-sparing walk and kept them moving steadily as they rode north.

"We saved a half day and a great deal of riding by taking that little swim," Ki said after they'd covered a mile or so in companionable silence. "We ought to get to the Locked O's just a little while before sunset."

"It'd help if we can get there before dark," Jessie nodded. "We can use the time to get an idea of the way the place is laid out. We didn't have a chance to see any details of it the night we stopped there."

"So we didn't," Ki agreed.

Jessie went on, "We might have to push the horses a bit, but it'll be worthwhile if we get there while there's still enough daylight to look it over."

"I'd say the horses can stand it. We haven't put much of a strain on them since we had to hurry away from the ranch the other night."

"There's one more reason to push a bit, Ki. Those two men who stopped at Joseph's Crossing yesterday were heading for the Locked O's. They might beat us there if we don't move fast. We already know we'll be outnumbered, but we aren't sure yet what the odds against us are going to be."

"Would it make any difference?" Ki smiled as he asked the question. "We'd still go ahead with our plan."

Jessie's sober, thoughtful expression gave way to a smile. She shook her head and replied, "Bad odds have never bothered us before, Ki. I don't suppose they will now."

Without any further discussion, they toed their mounts into a brisker pace. Except for the stretches where towering cliffs of forbidding-looking black basalt hills rose from the river's edge to hide Hell's Canyon from them, they could hear the rushing of the river at all times during their ride north. The awesome bulk of the dark humps on their left was a sharp contrast to the landscape on their right, where the gently rolling ground of the high prairie stretched to a far away horizon and the grass grew tall.

There were a few places along the road where the hills dipped and the roar of the river grew louder, and Jessie and Ki could get a glimpse of the Snake's tossing white water. During these short stretches when they could see the stream itself, the roar of its treacherous waters grew louder. But even during the long intervals when the river was hidden by humps and tilts of the hills and the broken sussurus of the wild waters in the canyon was little more than a whisper, there was never a moment when Jessie and Ki were unaware of its presence.

During the first hour of their ride the sun beat down on them with its merciless heat. Even at the moderate pace that they maintained the horses grew tired, and they stopped at shorter and shorter intervals to let them rest. At last the sun dropped behind the jagged western skyline that was never more than a long stone's throw from the trail. The heat diminished in the shade which now stretched across the narrow seldom-used trail, and they began to make better time.

"It's beginning to look like we're going to get to the Locked O's at just about the time that's best for us," Jessie remarked after they'd ridden up a long slope from a wide shallow valley that dipped below the forbidding black cliffs of the riverbed.

"That little line over there, the one that's just come into sight," Ki said, pointing ahead at the rim of the endless horizon. "It doesn't look like anything that nature ever created."

"But it does look like the top of that big barn behind the Locked O's," Jessie nodded after she'd studied the skyline for a moment.

"And we've certainly come far enough to be catching sight of the place," Ki agreed.

"Let's leave the trail, Ki, and circle around toward it."

Reining their horses off the beaten path, they moved ahead at a long diagonal to the east of the torturous path they'd been following along the rim of Hell's Canyon. Moving now in a straight line instead of following the curving trail that curved randomly in and out as it ran parallel to the canyon's rim, they pushed ahead at the same deliberate pace. After they'd covered a half-mile or so, Jessie turned to Ki.

"Do you miss it now, Ki, just like I do?" she asked.

"Miss what?"

"Why, the noise of the river."

"I miss the noise, but I'm glad it's gone," Ki observed. "The only thing I don't like too well is that we'll have to be a little more careful, now that we don't have the current's rush to cover any noises we might make."

Jessie had been glancing toward the canyon while Ki was answering her question. She gestured toward the east, where the sky was now beginning to take on the deeper hue of blue that promises nightfall.

"We're getting there at just the right time, too," she went on. "Another half-hour and the sun will be down."

Ki nodded. "We can get a little bit closer before there's any danger of one of the outlaws seeing us."

"Then the first good place we see that'll hide the horses, we'll stop."

"If there is a place like that in this area," Ki added. "We might have to wait until it's darker so we can walk the rest of the way without there being any danger that one of Plub Shattuck's gang will notice us."

They'd been pushing ahead slowly but steadily across the high-grassed ground while they planned. The roofline of the big two-story ranch house was plainly visible now. They rode only a short distance farther when the roof of the barn—almost as big and its roof only a little lower than that of the house—came into sight. As they rode on they could see that lights were already showing from a shedlike addition that had been built against the barn's side wall.

"Another half-mile and we'll be taking a risk we ought to avoid," Ki told Jessie.

"I know," she nodded. "But we're still quite a

long way from those buildings. I'd like to get closer."

"So would I, of course," Ki nodded. "But if we—" He broke off and stood up in his stirrups.

For a moment Ki studied the sweep of grassland that ran back from the canyon's rim. It was dotted here and there with small clumps of sage and a few small isolated scrub oak saplings, no higher than a man's shoulder. Then as he stretched and swept his eyes across the terrain again he found what they'd been hoping to see.

Looking down, he said, "Luck's with us, Jessie. There's a little clump of trees, scrub oak as nearly as I can tell, over a little way to the east of the big house."

"How far?"

"Not too far to go from there to the ranch house on foot as soon as it gets dark enough."

"Less than a quarter of a mile if I'm any judge of distance. And it's the only place I see where we could wait and watch without being noticed."

"Let's circle away from the ranch and head for them, then," Jessie said. "They just might give us the cover we need."

"They're a little too far away to be sure," Ki reported as he settled back into his saddle. "But from here I'd make a guess that they're just what we've been looking for."

Reining their horses to the right, they changed the angle of their approach to the outlaw hideout. Even in the changed direction they now were taking, they could still see the roofs of the Locked O's main house and the big barn behind it.

They covered another half-mile before the clump of scrub oak became visible, then once more changed the direction of their approach in order to be sure that during the time when they'd be riding directly toward the Locked O's the foliage of the trees would shield them from being seen by the outlaws.

Apparently the outlaws were busy, for while they were still approaching the tree-clump they glimpsed two men moving between the house and barn. They got only brief looks at the two, for the clump of trees that shielded them also kept them from getting a clear view of the two buildings.

"We couldn't've been luckier!" Jessie exclaimed as they drew closer to the half-dozen stunted oak saplings. "This is as safe a place as we can hope for to leave the horses."

"And as close," Ki added. "Now just as soon as it gets a bit darker, we'll go on to the house and see if we can find out how many of the men responsible for those senseless killings are still left."

They reached the little stand of low-branched trees and dismounted, led their horses to the edge of the cluster and tethered them. Then they stepped into the grove and dodged between the tree-trunks until they'd reached a point where to go any closer to the last few remaining between them and the house would have meant losing any concealment the tiny grove offered. They stopped their advance now and chose positions, then fixed their eyes on the Locked O's pair of buildings.

"Let's do our best to take them alive, Ki," Jessie said. "A trial in open court and a few hangings ought to keep anyone else from repeating that kind of senseless slaughter."

"You just said what I've been thinking," Ki told her. "Yes, Jessie. They'll all lie to us when we start asking questions, but one way or another, we'll find out."

They fell silent then, gazing steadily at the Locked O's main house. The sun's last red rays were beginning to fade from the western sky. The glow diminished rapidly. A surprisingly short time had slipped by between the time they'd begun their vigil to when the yellow glow of lamplight suddenly showed in the twin lower floor windows of the big house. Only moments later it was joined by a light from a smaller window in the upper story.

"They've either finished supper, or they're getting ready to eat now," Jessie remarked.

Ki glanced at the sky and said, "They won't be able to see anything with the lamps lit inside, even if they should happen to look out a window. I think it's time for use to start."

Jessie nodded silently. Side by side they stepped out of the live oak grove and moved toward the buildings. Even if they'd wanted to hide their approach there was no cover between them and the house, only the shin-high prairie grass and an occasional clump of knee-tall sage.

Above them the short twilight glow that had briefly kept the sky luminous was fading fast, giving way to the deeper blue of night and the gleams of stars. In the few minutes that passed while Jessie and Ki were moving toward the ranch buildings, the only sign of the ended day that broke the sudden darkness was a jagged thin pale blush-tinged line on the western horizon.

When only a few yards separated Jessie and Ki from the house Jessie said, her voice hushed, "Ki. Do you think we need a plan?"

"A plan for a situation that we can't foresee? We've tried plans before, and they've only worked a few times."

"I know. We'll improvise, as we always do, then."

A few more silent steps ahead brought them so near the window that they did not risk speaking again. Jessie pointed to the edge of the window on Ki's side as they got to the wall and moved to opposite sides of its frame as smoothly as though these had been prearranged positions. There were voices coming from the room beyond, and though neither window was open even a crack, the situation was identical with the one encountered during their earlier visit. The voices of the men talking inside the room were transmitted through the glass in a thin, tinny and almost inaudible whisper.

Jessie didn't recognize the voice that reached her ears. The speaker was saying, "... and you sure as hell don't keep a tight enough rein on your men, or those two that went down the canyon would've got back before dark, like you told 'em. Men that don't follow orders needs to be learned how to!"

"You got to remember things out here ain't like they are in town, Tim!" This time Jessie had no trouble in matching Plub Shattuck's name with the rasping bellowing voice. Shattuck went on, "There ain't no nice wide streets in Hell's Canyon like you got in town. And keep in mind that Bittman and Stilts had to get across the damn river twice! It might look easy, the way we work it, but that's still a nasty piece of water to fight!"

Quick anger tinged the voice of the man Shattuck addressed as Tim when he replied, "I don't need you to jog my memory, Plub! If you recall, I'm the one that found that place where we cross over the Snake, and I used it more'n once before you ever got here!"

"Don't get your dander blowed up so big it busts, Tim," Plub Shattuck said. His voice was calmer now, placating. "You don't aim to start back to Wallowa before morning. Bittman and Stilts will sure show up before then."

"They better!" Tim snapped. "And so had the two new men that're coming to replace the one that the Starbuck woman and her Chink flunkey killed. But if Bittman and Stilts did the job they were sent to do, we won't have to worry about those two any longer."

"You'll find they've done the job, and are likely on the way back, just running a little late. How many times do I have to tell you Bittman and Stilts are good as I made 'em out to be?"

"Till I see the proof they are," Tim replied in a sour voice. "Now where the devil are the men you've got left? I told you I'd want to talk to them a minute. They're going to have to answer a few questions."

"You already told me that, but you didn't get around to telling me why," Plub said. "They'll be here in a minute or so. I had Cookie hold up the fellows' supper a while because I figured Bittman and Stilts would be back before now."

"Well, they're not back, and the men that're here have had time to eat two suppers apiece," Tim growled. "You better go get 'em in here. Later on, I'll talk to the two that ain't back and the two new ones that're coming in. Now, before you go, I'm going to tell you just one thing more. I'm the boss here, and you're the one I pay to run things for me. When I tell you to do something, you better do it my way. You got that?"

"I've got it," Plub replied. "You've said the same thing before, and now I've heard it again. I ain't forgetting."

"Then roust the men in here, and I'll see if we can settle up the business I really come here on."

At their improvised listening-post outside the window, Jessie and Ki drew back and put their heads close together.

"Now we know who's really responsible for those killings in Hell's Canyon, Ki," she breathed. "I wonder if this Tim fellow is the sheriff Lily spoke of."

"We'll find out before we're through," Ki assured her. "And put his name on the top of the list, since he seems to've been the one who made the plans for the raid on the miners."

"As soon as we find out how many we're up against, we've got some plans of our own to make," Jessie said. "And we'll know a lot more than we did the first time we were—" She broke off as voices from the room they'd been watching reached them from the inside and said, "Let's get back to our window, Ki. I don't want to miss a word of what this fellow Tim has to say."

They resumed their places at the edges of the windows just in time to hear Tim begin.

"I've got a real big bone to pick with you men," he said. "You made a damned mess out of the job you did down in Hell's Canyon. You left one of the Chinks alive and either you didn't find all the gold pokes they had or you held back on me. It's taken me a while to catch up on this, but I'm here to get the whole thing straightened out. And don't make any mistake about it. The ones who're to blame are going to pay, or my name's not Tim Vetter!"

★

# Chapter 12

Jessie and Ki had the swift reflexes that belong to those who face danger often. However, the awkward sidewise-leaning positions which they'd been forced to twist into in order to peer through the small gaps at the edge of the window-shade had stiffened their muscles. They moved more slowly than usual.

Even before Jessie began turning away from the wall against which she'd been closely pressed, she glimpsed the swift motion of one of the outlaws drawing his revolver. The outlaw triggered his weapon while Vetter was still bringing up the muzzle of the sawed-off shotgun. The slug caught him in the shoulder, and although its impact spun him around in a half-turn, the heavy lead bullet failed to knock him down.

Somehow Vetter recovered from the bullet's impact. The shotgun's truncated muzzle had dropped. Though the wounded man was swaying, he managed to raise the muzzle level again. Another pistol slug tore into him.

After the second bullet hit, his knees began to buckle but his dying reflex tightened his finger around the twin triggers of the double-barrelled weapon. In the fraction of a second before his body began to sag, he somehow managed to close his finger on both the triggers. The shotgun's roar drowned the lighter reports from the six-guns of the outlaws who were still firing at the gang's leader. The slugs from the twin barrels remained in two almost-solid clumps as they flew through the narrow space between Vetter's sagging body and the kitchen range.

When the shotgun's massed slugs hit the cast-iron side of the stove its hot brittle metal cracked and broke. Only a few of the buckshot sailed through the breaks, but these were enough to scatter the flaming contents of the firebox.

Sprays of sparks and bits of the burning coals from the firebox scattered across the kitchen floor. Some of the blazing embers rolled into the room where the fracas had erupted. Small flickers of flame began dancing around the big cherry-red blobs of coal as the tinder-dry floorboards ignited.

Within seconds the dry wood of the floor was pocked with small flickers of flame dancing around each individual coal. The blazes were small for only an instant or two. They grew into knee-high tongues of flame that started spreading across the floor. The small flames at the edges of the individual spots of fire lengthened quickly and grew into spurting blazes that soared and rose knee-high.

"Let's go, Ki!" Jessie urged. "Those men will be getting out of there fast. We'd better find a place away from the fire, where they can't see us!"

Jessie turned and Ki followed her. Side by side they ran toward the sheltering darkness. Close behind them the ring of light cast by the fast-spreading fire followed them. They outran the glow and stopped at the edge of darkness to look back.

Only a few moments had passed since the fire began its lightning-fast spread. The window-shade had caught at once, and a few seconds later, the window burst with a loud pop that Jessie and Ki could hear above the crackle of the spreading conflagration.

Only two or three of the men they saw in the room showed any signs of thought beyond self-preservation, and these few began stamping at the flames in wild and futile dancing. One of them dived out the window. He landed on the hard ground head-first and sprawled unconscious, his prone figure motionless.

Inside the room, the men who'd been trying to stamp out the fires abandoned their efforts as the flames raced across its dry boards. Some of the outlaws tried to dash through the dancing tongues of fire that were now rising almost to the ceiling. Only one of them broke through, and he did not succeed in his effort to escape. Jessie and Ki could see his silhouetted form lurch forward and topple when he encountered the growing wall of dancing red tongues that now filled the kitchen.

On the ground beside the house the outlaw who'd dived head-first through the window stirred and picked himself up. He stood swaying for a moment as though he was about to collapse, then his head jerked up, and he took off in a limping run toward the big barn behind the burning house.

Shrouded in the protecting darkness, Jessie and Ki stood without speaking while they looked at the blaze. The fire had burst through the roof now on the side of the house where it had first started, and flickers were climbing up the walls.

They heard a sudden muffled roar and a shower of sparks shot high into the air. Most of the sparks died quickly, but enough reached the roof of the barn to land on it. Where the sparks survived and glowed only moments passed before they'd become patches of flame that edged rapidly along the shingled roof.

"In another few minutes, there won't be anything left of the Locked O's," Jessie told Ki. Her tone was sober, it held no hint of satisfaction or gloating.

"Or Vetter's outlaw gang either," Ki said. His voice was as expressionless as Jessie's had been. "He died fast, and I'm sure there are others who couldn't get out in time."

"I hate to be heartless, Ki," Jessie went on. "But I don't feel at all inclined to offer them any help."

"Neither do I," Ki agreed. "I can't forget that those men are the ones who slaughtered the people in Hell's Canyon."

"Somehow, I feel that even if we offered to help,

men who're as heartless as they are would be in-clined to shoot us instead of welcoming our help."

They fell silent then. Above the muted roar of the flames, shouts were now coming from the burning barn. Rising over the crackles and shouts, the shrill frantic neighing of frightened horses was cutting through the smoke-filled air. Jessie and Ki could not see what was happening, but they knew that the outlaws were trying to save their horses and gear.

"They're going to be busy for a long time," Ki commented.

"Yes," Jessie nodded, then she went on, "I suppose we could ride right past them without being noticed, but we'd better keep in the open country beyond the fire's light and get back to the road."

"We won't have to ride much further tonight, Jessie. Only a few miles after we get to the road. Then we can stop and sleep and go on to Joseph's Crossing in the morning."

Turning their backs on the burning buildings, they walked in silence to the horses and mounted. They let the rested animals pick their own way across the open country, touching the reins only occasionally to guide their mounts in a wide arc beyond the glare of the flames that still lighted the sky and marked the end of the outlaw headquarters.

Even before they reached the road, they could hear the muted rushing of the Snake River rising from Hell's Canyon. The ever-changing sound of the wildly roaring river stayed with them until sleep and rest could no longer be postponed. They pulled off the road and found a spread of thick high grass far enough away from the road to shield them from discovery.

Both Jessie and Ki were exhausted. Once asleep, cradled in a stand of tall grass with nothing to disturb them but the low whispers of the vagrant wind rustling the grass, they slept soundly. When dawn crept up from the east and a faint light began to spread across the prairie, they continued to sleep. The dawn brightened, then the sun began its slow rise, bringing with it a brisk but intermittent breeze that rustled the grass-tips, and still they slept.

As faint as the hoofbeats were, and as distant from the trail as was the place where they'd bedded down, Jessie and Ki snapped wide awake when the distant thunking of hooves broke the sunrise stillness. Ki sat up, and almost before he'd raised his head, Jessie was also starting to sit up in her blankets. They listened for a few moments, their eyes toward the trail, but as yet the approaching riders were out of sight.

"I think we both know who those riders are," Jessie told Ki after they'd sat silently for a moment or two.

"Yes, they've got to be the pair that stopped at Joseph's Landing to visit with the ferryman. Do you think we ought to do anything about them?"

"No, I don't think so, Ki," she replied thoughtfully. "The grass will hide us, all we have to do is lie down again. They'll be watching the trail, and I'm sure they'll ride right on past."

"They're certainly not going to be any threat to us . . . or anybody else, for quite a while," Ki said. "They're going to find a mess at the Locked O's that'll take a long time to clean up, if they decide to stay there."

"I doubt that anybody's going to stay there very long. The house and barn aren't anything but ashes by now."

"I'm sure that Tim Vetter's dead," Ki went on. "And he was the brains. Plub Shattuck's more than likely dead, too. Whatever's left of the gang will just move on."

"And moving will scatter them," Jessie agreed. "Besides, we're more than halfway to the landing now."

"Suppose we just lie back down and wait until they pass, then."

"That's our best bet," Jessie nodded. "We'll give them plenty of time to get out of earshot, then we'll go on to Joseph's Landing."

"After we have a bite of breakfast," Ki amended, "I feel like I haven't eaten anything for a week."

"Daylight and breakfast and a clear trail ahead certainly makes a lot of difference in the way you look at a day," Jessie said to Ki as they let their horses set their own pace along the path.

They were out of sight of the river but not out of earshot. The gurgles of its angry current still reached them in spite of the forbidding black basalt formation that rose high above their heads and hid the canyon's depths and formed an effective barrier between the trail and the stream.

"Yes. Last night seems something like a bad dream," Ki agreed. "And we're not very far from Joseph's Landing now."

Jessie nodded, and for the next three-quarters of a mile, they said nothing while around them the landscape underwent the sudden changes to which they'd almost become accustomed. For the past few miles they'd been riding with the rolling prairie on one side of the path and the forbidding black rock shoulder of Hell's Canyon's gorge on the other. The voice of the river continued to fill the breezeless mid-morning air, and even though they could not see its dark eddying flow, the sound kept them constantly aware of its presence.

"Another half-hour, and we'll be on the flats again," Jessie remarked after they'd ridden a while longer. "And I think that if I never see this black rock again I'll be just as happy."

Jessie got her wish in part, for another quarter of an hour of steady riding brought them to the point where the basalt shoulder began tapering downward into the sandy soil. Where earth and rock met, the character of the ground began to change into the softer, loose dirt that marked the beginning of a stretch of flatland. When the trail curved toward the river they could see its wide span as it flowed almost unrippled between the two broad stretches of sandy soil that now formed its banks.

"There's the ferryman's shack," Jessie said as they came in sight of the little shanty and the ferryboat swaying at its mooring. "We'll be on the other side of the river soon, and right now that's almost equal to being on the way back home."

A few more minutes brought them to the ferrylanding. Frank Smith came out of his shack when he heard the hoofbeats of their horses and started walking toward them as they dismounted.

"I wasn't looking for you to come back on this bank of the river," he said. "You been down to Pittsburg Landing?"

Ki looked at Jessie and though his face remained expressionless she knew that he was waiting for her to reply to Smith's question.

"We found a place where we thought we could swim our horses across," she replied straightfaced. "And we were right. It wasn't easy, but we managed."

"Well, I sure hope you don't go talking about it too much," the ferryman frowned. "If folks figure they can git across without paying no fare, I might have to close down the ferry."

"We won't be here long enough to tell anyone, except Lily," Jessie said. "So you won't have to worry."

"Didn't pass nobody on the road, I guess?"

"We heard some riders go by where we'd stopped away from the road to sleep, but we didn't see them," Ki volunteered.

"Heading south? That'd be them two fellows that stopped to visit me. Don't reckon they seen you, either, from what you just said."

"No, as Ki told you, we only heard their horses," Jessie assured him.

"Well, now. I guess I better get moving and haul you folks across," Smith went on.

He pulled in the little gangplank and began levering the ferry across the stream. Ki paid the fare while they were crossing, and he and Jessie wasted no time in leading their mounts ashore. They rode

167

up the slope the short distance to Lily Smith's small house and reined in. Before either Jessie or Ki could dismount, Moy-Tae-On rushed out the door.

"Jessie! Ki!" she exclaimed. "So glad I am to see you!"

"But we haven't been gone very long," Jessie smiled. Then she saw how sober Moy-Tae-On's expression had suddenly become and went on, "And . . . well, I'm afraid we don't have any encouraging news about your people."

"I did not really expect any, Jessie," Moy-Tae-On said. "I knew all that I could do was hope."

"We do have something for you though." Ki tried to put a cheerful note into his voice, but seeing Moy-Tae-On had recalled the deserted camp of the Orientals, his effort was only partly successful.

"Something? What sort of something?" she asked.

Ki had turned to his horse to get the gold poke from his saddlebag and did not answer at once. As he turned back he held up the bulging leather poke and said, "Gold, Moy-Tae-On. It is gold your friends got from the riverbed. At least you'll have money to start a different kind of new life in America."

"Thank you, Ki. And you, too, Jessie," Moy-Tae-On said as she took the sack that Ki was holding out for her. "I did not look for good news or really for anything. But now I know I have friends and a way to start again."

Lily suddenly appeared in the doorway. "Well, Jessie! You and Ki come on in and set in something besides a saddle for a change! We wasn't to say ex-

168

pecting you, but we're sure glad you're back safe. While you're resting up, I'll get supper started. Then we'll just set and palaver, and when you're too tired to talk any more, we'll go to bed. You'll get a good night's sleep on something besides hard ground!"

"Go with Lily," Moy-Tae-On said to Jessie. "I will help Ki with the horses."

Jessie nodded and turned back to Lily. "I hope your coffeepot's on the stove," she smiled. "I could use a cup before we sit down to eat."

"And you'll have one," Lily told her. As she and Jessie started inside she dropped her voice and went on, "I figured Moy better have a minute or so to talk with Ki. I don't reckon you found much except that gold poke?" As she spoke, her eyebrows went up questioningly.

Jessie shook her head. "No. But we did have a run-in with the outlaws at the Locked O's."

Lily went on, "I'm sorry about you and Ki having trouble, Jessie. Maybe I ought've told you more, but I been sorta edgy about that bunch. I'm too old to get hurt much more, and from what I seen of you and Ki, I figured you was growed-up enough to look after yourselves."

"I think we did," Jessie said. "We didn't make a clean sweep of the gang, but they won't be bothering you. Now, let's have that coffee. We can talk about what's happened while we're eating supper. I'm ready for some home cookin'!"

★

# Chapter 13

"That was certainly a delicious dinner, Lily," Jessie said as they sat sipping tea after their meal. "But I'm afraid we've put you to a lot of trouble."

"Don't let that worry you a minute, Jessie," Lily replied. "It ain't very frequent I got real company like you and Ki and Moy-Tae-On. But now we've had supper, I got to say I don't have no ideas about how we're all going to sleep tonight, since I only got one bed."

"I have been thinking, too," Moy-Tae-On said quickly. "It is easy to answer what you have said, Lily. You are the elder, and Jessie is guest. You will have the bed. I will make Chinese bed on floor, Ki will, too."

"Even that's going to make the room crowded," Ki put in. "I'll spread my bedroll outside. When I

171

took care of the horses, I left it out by the door so it would be handy."

"Now, you can't do that, Ki!" Lily protested. "When I got a visitor, I like for 'em to have a proper place to sleep."

"Let Ki have his way, Lily," Jessie advised. "He'll do what he wants to, anyhow."

"Well—" Lily began hesitantly.

Ki broke in before she could go on, "Jessie knows my stubborn Oriental habits, Lily. She's right, you know."

"I guess it'd be wasting breath to say anything else, then," Lily told them. "And since you two had a real long ride getting here, I don't imagine you'll feel like setting up much longer, palavering with me and Moy-Tae-On. Whenever you say, we can start getting ready to bed down."

"Let's not put it off, then," Jessie suggested.

Standing up, Ki said, "I'll cast my vote with Jessie. We have had a busy day and a long ride. I will bid you good night and go to my own rest."

Ki wasted no time in taking the straps off his bedroll and spreading it around the corner from the door, where the house would shield him from the prevailing cool wind that blew from the river. He slid out of his loose jacket and trousers and rolled them together, laid the roll at one end of the blankets and slid the case containing his *shuriken* under the edge of the make-shift pillow.

Then he stepped out of his slippers and slid between the blankets. He lay awake for only a few minutes, listening to the murmur of the women talking and laughing inside, then slipped into a sound sleep.

How long he'd slept Ki did not know when a hand closed over his mouth. He reacted by instinct even as his eyes were opening. His hand shot from beneath the covers and closed on the wrist of whoever was disturbing him, while at the same time, he rolled on his side to free his knee from the blankets covering him in the beginning of a *hiza geri* knee-kick.

Then he used all of the finely-honed muscular control at his command to stop the kick before his knee met flesh when Moy-Tae-On's quick whisper reached his ears.

"No, Ki!" she breathed. "It is only me!"

"Aie!" Ki whispered. "I am sorry, Moy-Tae-On."

"No, the fault is mine," she replied in the same hushed tone. "I should have spoken to wake you before I touched you."

"Is something wrong?" he asked.

"No. Unless I have been wrong in seeking you in your bed."

"It is not wrong if you wanted to come to me," Ki told her. He lifted the blanket and went on, "I'm surprised, but I am also pleased. Come lie with me."

Moy-Tae-On shrugged off the thin night-shift she was wearing. Ki caught a quick glimpse of the dark nipples on her small rounded breasts and of the dark triangle of her pubic brush as she slid under the blanket beside him.

"I did not intend to join you until tomorrow night, but when Jessie told me that you were leaving at daybreak tomorrow, I knew that I could not let this night pass by."

"This is something you wanted to do?" Ki asked. He had made no move to embrace Moy-Tae-On, though her warm skin was pressed against him.

"Of course. If it hadn't been, I would not be here, even though many weeks have passed since I lay with a man."

"If it is your wish and not payment that you might think you should offer for a debt you imagine, I'm very glad."

"It is you I want, Ki. Ever since my hunger-weakness left me, I have been thinking of you."

While she was talking, Moy-Tae-On's hand was exploring Ki's crotch. She fingered him gently with an exploring hand, and Ki let himself begin an erection. Moy-Tae-On stroked his swelling shaft gently for a few moments before grasping his wrist with her free hand and guiding it into the vee of her thighs. Ki no longer held back the completion of his erection but allowed himself to swell in response to the teasing pleasure of her caressing fingertips.

Moy-Tae-On spread her thighs as she continued the subtle movements of her fingers, and Ki began the masculine version of her fingertip caresses. Moy-Tae-On's small body began to quiver as they prolonged their pleasures. Ki brought his control into full play as his shaft reached its swollen full-ness, and she brought into use the subtle pressures, releases and silken sweeps of her hands.

At last Moy-Tae-On whispered softly, "It is time now, Ki. I am as ready for you as you are for me."

Ki kneeled above her now and entered her moist

waiting warmth with the same slow deliberation that had marked their foreplay. Moy-Tae-On knew the responses. She used the pressure of her foot-soles on his hips to accept his slow penetration or hold him from going further while all the time Ki was caressing the tips of her budded breasts with his iron-hard fingertips.

Time did not matter to them now. They continued their foreplay until the gentle caresses no longer satisfied them. Moy-Tae-On's small body was beginning to tremble. Ki recognized the moment and completed his penetration with a quick forceful thrust that brought a gasp of pleasure from Moy-Tae-On's lips.

Once he'd begun his deep quick thrusts Ki knew there was no further restraint that would increase their pleasure. He drove fully now with each lunge until the quivering of Moy-Tae-On's small supple body and the gasps that pulsed from her lips told him that she was as ready as he was.

Ki pounded now, and she met his lunges with twists of her rocking hips. They were lost to the world as their rhythms increased until they could move no faster. Then Moy-Tae-On cried out, a small stifled scream, and Ki thrust with the final deep and almost fierce penetrations that brought him to his own peak. Moy-Tae-On could no longer stifle the cries in her throat, she pulled Ki's lips to hers to muffle her loud scream. Ki pressed his hips against hers and held himself poised there. They clung together while shudders raced through their taut bodies. They shivered through the climactic instants that came with completion.

"I was sure you would be a good lover, Ki," Moy-Tae-On whispered into Ki's ear as his head rested on her shoulder. "I would have come to you before, but I needed to gain strength and to rest so I could please you. I did please you, didn't I?"

"Of course you did. And will again. Soon."

They let satisfied silence speak for them then, and Ki was beginning to grow sleepy when a distant grating of metal on metal reached his ears. It was no more than a whisper, but the noise was alien to the night. He lifted his head to listen. After a few moments the noise was repeated, and now Ki rose to his knees in spite of the pressure of Moy-Tae-On's clinging arms. He now recongized the source of the metallic clinking, it was the sound of the lever that propelled the ferryboat striking the taut cable as it crossed from shore to shore.

"Did you hear it, Moy-Tae-On?" he asked.

"Of course. Listening while I was alone and afraid in the canyon has made my ears very sharp. It is the ferryboat crossing the river, that is all."

"It's enough," Ki said. "The ferry should not be crossing at this time of the night." He was juggling time-frames in his mind now. He went on, "Hurry and dress. Go inside and wake Jessie. Tell her to show no light, and to bring her rifle and pistol and all the shells she has for both."

"Rifle? Shells? You think there will be fighting, here? In the darkness?"

"I know there will," Ki assured her soberly. "And don't try to help in it, Moy-Tae-On. Stay inside the cabin with Lily. Jessie and I can handle this.

Now, get her for me at once. We don't have much time to get ready."

Moy-Tae-On did not question Ki again. She reached for her slip and shrugged into it as she was moving toward the door. Ki dressed quickly and groped for his saddlebags in the gloom. He took out his reserve supply of *shuriken*, but did not remove their oiled silk wrapping before tucking them into the capacious pocket of his loose black jacket.

He heard the creak of the cabin door, then Jessie's voice. She called in a voice little above a whisper, "Ki? Where are you?"

"Here." Ki waited, listening. He heard the faint scuff of Jessie's boots, but the noises from the river had stopped.

Jessie reached his side and whispered, "What's happening, Ki? Moy-Tae-On said there's trouble."

"I heard the ferry crossing, Jessie. Frank Smith wouldn't be coming to this side of the river alone at this time of night."

Jessie connected Ki's words at once with their fight at the Locked O's. She asked, "The men who passed us on the road?" Without waiting for Ki to reply she went on, "Of course. They've had plenty of time to get to the Locked O's and come back with the outlaws who're still alive."

"And they're here now to get their revenge. They had to be the ones who just crossed on the ferry. I'm sure Smith works closely with them. He couldn't live on fares from the few people who'd want to cross the river here."

Jessie saw the logic of Ki's assumptions. They'd learned many things during the long years spent battling the cartel, and both knew how the minds of the lawless work.

"Do you think they'll attack in the dark?" she asked. "Or will they wait until dawn?"

"It's almost dawn now. Daylight will give them an edge. But they know the lay of the land, so they might start before dawn. They're probably moving right now to surround the cabin, and I'd guess they'll be coming at us from all sides."

"Then we'll do what we always do in a situation like this," Jessie said quickly. "Guard the corners."

"Yes," Ki agreed. "You take the front corner, there's not much cover between here and the river. I'll look after the back corner between here and the trees."

They made no further plans. Experience had taught both that even the best of plans made before a fight begins must be changed to meet unexpected moves by the enemy. Jessie started for the corner of the house that pointed toward the ferry crossing. Ki moved the few steps required to reach his station.

He looked into the gloom. Night still held on, and the blackness on all sides was silent. Ki realized at once that he had no choice but to wait until one of their attackers moved carelessly and made a noise. He knew that even the slight whispering rasp of cloth or a hand brushing on tree bark, or the grating of a bootsole on a rock would reach him in the darkness. Regardless of the direction in which he turned his head, the blackness was totally silent.

Jessie was painfully aware of the grating of her feet on the hard soil as she moved with slow careful steps along the wall of Lily's small house to the corner nearest the river. She gazed toward the water. A few glitters of starlight could be seen reflecting from the rushing waters, but they were too small to give off any light. They appeared only at long intervals where the roiling surface flowed clear in short streaks before it bubbled over a rock or a riffle of bottom sand.

She waited patiently, aware of the streaks of silver that had now begun to outline the horizon at each end of her field of vision. Experience in other night-watches had taught her that the streaks would widen quickly, until they merged into an arc of predawn grey. When the river began to reflect the merging streaks, anything between her and the water would quickly become silhouetted and an easy target.

Jessie reassured herself that the tiny glitters of the stars had begun to disappear in the brighter glow of the before-sunrise sky. The small bright streaks on the dark surface of the stream widened quickly. Jessie began scanning the expanse between the house and the river.

She could see the boat at the ferry landing outlined against the river now. After glancing at it, she shifted her position a few inches to widen her field of view. Her unplanned move may have saved her life. A rifle cracked, a spurt of muzzle-blast cut a red streak and a bullet thunked into the wall where her head had been.

Her rifle was ready in her hands. Jessie fired at the spot where she'd seen the streak, bracketing the target in rapid-fire and pumping fresh shells into her rifle's chamber with the speed and skill that only an expert acquires. Her third shot brought a yowl of pain from the semidark slope of the riverbank, and the dark silhouette of a man appeared for an instant against the brightening surface of the Snake. The black figure remained poised erect for a moment, then pitched forward and lay still.

As though the barking of Jessie's rifle had been a signal, the blackness in the grove of trees that Ki faced behind the cabin was cut by red spurts of muzzle-blast. Before the sound of the first shot had died away, Ki looked for a target. He saw no sign of movement for several minutes. Then a black shape separated itself from the lesser blackness of the brightening day and began dodging from tree to tree, moving toward the cabin.

Ki stepped back into the darkness of the cabin's projecting corner and waited. His wait was short. The dark form showed again for a few seconds before it was hidden by another tree. Ki had his target now, and a *shuriken* was in his hand.

He saw the shadowy form break the straight tapering outline of a tree trunk, waited a moment, and sent the razor-edged blade whirling toward the darkly outlined man. The attacker saw the shimmer of the *shuriken*'s points too late. Before he could dodge or raise a hand the steel bit into his throat and severed his jugular. The man pawed at the blade, but the rush of his lifeblood could not be stopped. He sagged and sprawled and lay still.

• • •

Jessie was busy now. Two shadowed forms had appeared on the barren strip between the cabin and the river. They were perfect targets, outlined sharply against the brightening water. Jessie swung her rifle from one to the other. She took her time, making sure of her aim before squeezing off her shots. Five bullets disposed of the two within as many minutes.

Ki stepped back into the black shadow at the cabin's corner when the advancing man crumpled. He heard a scraping of boot-soles and turned, *shuriken* in hand, in the direction from which the noise came.

A man's voice broke the silence. "Zeb?" he called, his voice puzzled. "Zeb? Where'n hell are you?"

Ki provided the reply. He swivelled to face the direction from which the call had come and saw the man who'd called moving toward the cabin with long steps. The newcomer target stopped when he saw the sprawled form of the man he'd been seeking, and the stop signed his doomsday warrant.

Ki took the opportunity without delay. His throwing-blade was whirling to its target when the man among the trees raised his head and turned to look toward the cabin. The *shuriken* cut into ear, and one of its needle-sharp points pierced the small fragile bones behind his ear and dug into his brain. He stood motionless for a moment, then dropped as though the *shuriken* had been a poleax.

Again Ki backed into the shadows and waited, but there was no sound from the trees. They were outlined now against the brightening sky, and though Ki examined the entire stretch of the scattered pine grove, he saw no signs of life, no moving shadows or shapeless forms. Then Jessie's quick shots broke the silence, and Ki moved quickly around the side of the cabin to look for her.

Jessie had not left the concealment of the shadow, though the steadily-brightening light was diminishing the effectiveness of her position. She looked questioningly at Ki.

"Do you think there were only five of them?" she asked.

"More than likely," he nodded.

"You're probably right, at that," she said thoughtfully. "The two men who passed us going to the Locked O's and three of the outlaws who survived the fire."

"Maybe some of the others came out of it alive, but weren't able to travel," Ki suggested.

"But the gang's broken," Jessie pointed out. "So we—"

Lily's voice from the cabin door interrupted Jessie. "We ain't heard any shooting for a while. Can me and Moy-Tae-On come out now?"

"Yes," Jessie replied. "You don't have to worry, Lily."

Lily and Moy-Tae-On emerged from the cabin, blinking in the brightening daylight.

Jessie said, "Ki and I were just talking about leaving, Moy-Tae-On. I'm sure you'll be glad to get away from here, too."

For a moment the young Chinese girl said nothing, then she told Jessie, "I do not think I wish to go anywhere, Jessie. I have nothing anywhere else."

"But your bad memories of Hell's Canyon—" Ki began.

"Will fade with time, Ki."

"Moy-Tae-On is right, Ki," Jessie said. "She'll find peace in her own way. And we've got business waiting for us. I think we can be ready to start back in an hour or so, don't you?"

"Of course. And I'm sure that you'll be as glad as I am to get out of Hell's Canyon."